"While her protagon
McKee imbues their s
      something uplifting out of terrible
          circumstances."

— Self-Publishing Review, July 2016.

Girl Imperilled by Ellie Rose McKee
www.ellierosemckee.com

Copyright © 2023 Ellie Rose McKee

ISBN: 978-1-8384323-5-5

Girl Imperilled

A Short Story Collection
by Ellie Rose McKee

WWW.ELOWENPRESS.COM

Also by Ellie Rose McKee

Author Note

Trigger warnings are listed on the back page of this book, to be read in advance—or ignored—at the reader's discretion.

Contents

Drawbacks

Cara was done with life. But, to be fair, life had seemed done with her first. Fate had found her a husband—someone she'd loved with all she had—only for him to walk away when fate had also made it impossible for her to bear the troupe of children he'd wanted. No, expected. Demanded, almost.

And now, unable to cope with her wretched existence any longer, Cara was giving herself to the sea.

She was successfully failing to keep her head above water when suddenly it was gone. Her body was thrown against sand and rock. The force and shock of no longer being buffeted by the tide shoved air back into her.

Cara hacked up lungfuls of brine as her salt-stinging eyes scanned the now-empty beach. Several hundred feet of seabed was now uncovered as water retreated away from land. She would have thought it a lifesaving miracle, but she'd heard about this phenomenon before.

In fact, she was pretty sure she'd half-glanced at an article about it while she'd been on the plane, on her way to this place she'd always wanted to see. This place she'd chosen as the last one she'd ever see.

Something inside her twisted. Something instinctual, well beyond herself or her own understanding. The blood in her veins was screaming, a single word: *run.*

Hauling herself up on aching legs, Cara tore up the beach. Towards grass. Towards life. Lactic acid in her muscles burned but she didn't let up until she reached the lobby of a fancy hotel towering high.

A flock of tourists were glued to the window, marvelling at the strange view of the sea running away, with yet more going outside to take photos. Staff were trying to herd some of them, and Cara tried yelling a warning of her own, but it made no difference.

The receptionist looked frozen with fear and the security guard lost to resignation as Cara passed them both and punched the button for the lift.

The doors opened and she leapt in, heart slamming in her chest.

The glass elevator began its climb to the top as Cara watched the sea turn and begin its return journey inland, gathering speed. Terror flooded every cell in her body as the realisation dawned that if anyone else called the lift—if she didn't reach the very top very, very soon—she would never get there at all.

The elevator rose. The light for each floor passed without pausing.

Cara held her breath.

The doors opened.

She ran out onto the flat roof as the tsunami swept around the building, almost licking the edge.

And Cara looked out over the water, the only thing alive for miles.

Earworms

The noise was driving him mad. No, *worse* than mad. It was driving him so far around the bend he couldn't think crooked, let alone straight—not even enough to find a word for just how crazy the sound made him.

It hadn't been so bad at first—just some catchy tune. For an hour or so, Kipling couldn't see what all the fuss was about this whole music lark. It was fun, not something that should be banned or "treated" as fast as possible.

That was then.

Now, ten hours into his torture, the novelty had well and truly worn off. And Kipling had been so confident that it wouldn't, he hadn't told anyone, and now it was too late to get the extraction procedure.

The music had become static as the earworm buried deeper into his skull and embedded itself. Now he didn't need to tell anyone, because Clara was walking up to him with a resigned look and there was no doubt in Kipling's mind that she already knew.

"How goes it?" she asked in that slow, steady cadence she had.

It had always got on Kipling's nerves, but he especially couldn't stand it now. She always talked like she knew everything, but he'd never bought it. And now that he could tell she really did know something, she was insulting him by playing dumb? It boiled his blood.

Kipling couldn't answer. An idea taking over him just as much as the sound. A terrible, treacherous idea that grew increasingly attractive the more he looked into Clara's dull eyes and stupid face.

Rumour had it, she'd had earworms, once—not just one, but an infestation. They had caught her while she was asleep, and it had been too late for surgery by the time she'd woken up and figured out what was wrong.

The townsfolk said she'd lived with it longer than anyone else, and they revered her for it, but Kipling didn't. To him, it didn't matter how long she'd endured, because everyone knew that outside of surgery, the only way to get rid of earworms was to pass them on. And here she was, still living her life, so she'd clearly been just as weak as the rest of them in the end, surrendering to temptation and passing the affliction on just to be free.

A smug feeling crept over Kipling as he thought about just how *right* it would be to have her suffer the reality of *his* earworm, which surely had to be worse than any she'd had. If indeed she'd had any at all. He could just imagine her having lied about it—to impress someone, maybe, before word had inadvertently gotten out—so far and so fast she couldn't bear to admit the lie. If that was the case, he'd been right to have always mistrusted her, and she deserved to be taught a lesson.

Kipling would show her what it was to suffer.

"I'm just swell, Clara," he said at last, his voice sounding oily even to his own ears.

His own damn, incessantly chiming ears. Hell, at this point, he didn't even care if she deserved to be infected or not, he just needed space in his head again, and what better way?

As he leaned close to her, as if about to share a secret, the worm inside his head squirmed. He resisted the urge to flinch. Supposedly, you just got real close to someone else and it would jump host from the old to the new. Why wasn't anything happening?

"Kipling," she said, warning in her voice. And he knew—knew that she'd figured out his plan and was going to try and stop him. He wouldn't have it. She was old, and he was fast.

With sweating palms and pounding heart, Kipling grabbed Clara's shoulders and leaned closer still. The worm in his head writhed manically and Clara gasped. The edge of his vision darkened and a rushing sound filled his head, the whirlwind of what had to be at least four or five hundred beasts leaving her head and swirling towards his ears. He felt the original worm in his head as it screamed and died at the influx of creatures.

The cacophony of noise congealed into a wall of sound, blocking everything else out until he could hear only white noise. Beside him, Clara fell to her knees. She was opening and closing her mouth, and had pure terror in her eyes, but he couldn't hear her screams over the hurricane in his own head.

Kipling saw the town surgeon come running. He went to Clara first, but even in her distress, she gestured for him to help Kipling first.

His vision darkened further as the surgeon leaned over him, and all he could think was, *wrong. I was so wrong. How in the hell did she live like this?*

Kipling just couldn't imagine it. Or what she must be feeling now, finally being free of so much noise after so long.

Clara's face was the last thing he saw as he passed out.

Defence

"It wasn't my fault," said Janet. "It was not! They'll try and tell you that I did it, but they're lying. I would never lie. My mother made sure of that. *Tell the truth*, she'd say, *or it'll be slapped legs*. I learned that lesson early on, at least ten times.

"Burnt fingers never forget.

"So, you see? It couldn't have been me.

"What about Brian, or Muriel? I don't think they know the right way of things at all, or else why would they lie about me? It must have been one of them.

"In fact, I think I saw Brian in the room just before it happened. Not that I was there, of course. I saw him leave. Yeah, that was it. I saw him walk out of the room before the district manager walked into it and made the discovery. Because I was outside the room, see? Watching the door as they walked through it, that's all I ever did. If anything, that should make me the star witness, not the accused.

"I was never in the room. In fact, I don't even know what's in the room, because I've never seen it. Never. That's how innocent I am. How could it be me if I was never there? It couldn't. There. Point proven, case closed. It was so very obviously Brian who did it."

The line manager walked around the table towards her and sat perched on the edge.

"Janet," he said, looking down at her.

She looked down at her hands.

"Janet," he said again, then cleared his throat.

She bit her lip, then looked up at him. "Yes?"

He paused as if looking into her soul. "Janet, enough of this now. Did you do it?"

She looked down at her hands again. They were shaking.

"Yes," she admitted at last. "I did it. I ate the last slice of cake."

Prepared

Enough was enough. Lynette could put off sorting through her baggage no longer. She needed to be prepared, so she would do this. If she did this, it would all be okay.

She climbed the ladder, opened the hatch in the ceiling, and stuck her head in, instantly overwhelmed by the task ahead of her. The attic was bigger than she remembered. Fuller and darker, too. Lynette had to run downstairs for a lamp and come back up again.

There. That was better. At least she could see to make a start.

Preparation, she reminded herself. That was the key. She'd been focusing on it like a mantra, almost as if doing so would in itself get her ready. But she knew better. Knew the real solution was in the practical.

Soon, she'd have to deal with her mother, and Lynette promised herself she'd have her shit together by the time that inevitable nightmare arrived.

First, there was a box of old Christmas tat. The tree lights were tangled and bulbs were blown. The tinsel had all but fallen apart, and the candy canes were several years out of date. Unfortunate, but she supposed it made things easier.

Lynette threw the box through the hatch, creating a pile for the dump, and lifted the next in line: a plastic container full of old phone books. Well, those could go as well. Maybe the whole job would be this easy, and she'd been worrying about nothing.

One by one, Lynette opened the rest of the boxes and tossed them aside. She was ready to call it a day, dust her hands off and climb back through the hatch when her eye caught one final box shoved away in the darkest corner. It took some doing—crawling on her hands and knees to get over to it, and using all her strength to pull it out of the too-tight nook it was in—but, finally, Lynette dislodged the box and brought it closer to the light.

She flipped open the lid and began to cough at all the dust flying about. Then, when she had her breath back and the dust cloud had cleared, Lynette gasped.

This. This was exactly the kind of thing she'd wanted to avoid.

Inside the box, thousands of eyes from thousands of loose, faded photos stared out at her: her mother's eyes from her first communion; her mother's eyes on her mother's wedding day, and Lynette's wedding day; and her mother's eyes as they sat on the beach, Lynette playing in the sand.

The eyes cold. Sad. In each and every single one.

Lynette was tempted to tip the photos out with all the rest, but she couldn't. Of course she couldn't. She'd come this far, so she might as well finish.

Dragging the box out of the attic, Lynette turned off the lamp and closed the hatch. With some effort, she carried all of the stuff for the dump down to the garage, where she could bribe some of the neighbourhood kids to take it the rest of the way.

Then, with nothing more to distract herself with, Lynette took the box of photographs into the living room with her. She poured herself a glass of wine and sat down to work. First, she had to sort the snapshots by the dates on the back. Then she could painstakingly stick them into photo albums. It would take weeks, she feared, and probably more than a dozen albums. She'd resent her mum for that, annoyed that there had been so many photos taken when she clearly didn't want to be in any of them, except Lynette knew it was her dad's doing, and Lynette could absolutely never resent her father.

Several hours and half a bottle of wine later, Lynette at least had the photos in chronological order. She picked up the last in the stack—the most recent—a candid shot of Lynette and her mother at some birthday or other. Because it wasn't posed like all the rest, it had a nice quality that Lynette found she actually liked. She was thinking about framing it, wondering where she would hang it, when the phone ringing startled her.

Slowly Lynette got up and padded over to the phone. The wine had unsteadied her a little, but one look at the clock did a lot to sober her up.

Four A.M.

No good news ever came at four in the morning.

Lynette swallowed and lifted the receiver to her ear. The person on the other end started talking without her having to say hello. They were polite and direct and succinct.

Lynette wanted to scream at them. She wanted to scream at herself, and her mother. Instead, she nodded along and set the phone down when the person on the other side had finished. Had they said they were a nurse? Or a doctor? Lynette didn't remember. Already, most of the conversation had become a fog in her mind, with only the two key words sticking out, clear as day:

She's gone.

Lynette sank to her knees, sending the photographs scattering—all of her hard work for nothing. Like a fool, she'd thought she could deal with death before it happened. Nip grief off in the bud. But, at the end of the day, she wasn't the least bit prepared.

Quest

The most skilled warrior in her land, Adira was called in to deal with the threat. It was a big threat, she was told. Perhaps the biggest she'd ever faced, the Leader had said.

At first, she was dubious. She'd dealt with a lot of foes in her time—trojans and thieves and, once, even terrorists—all of which had been initially considered out of her league. But the Leader was insistent that Adira take great caution, and not be overconfident. This threat—a group of trolls––was not particularly numerous, but they were nasty and had already caused a great deal of damage.

Previous warriors had all failed to defeat them, and it was becoming increasingly vital that the trolls were vanquished, as they had formed their lair underneath the main trading route and had majorly disrupted the day-to-day lives of the residents, attacking without mercy. Seemingly without rhyme or reason.

The people were suffering, and Adira was their only hope.

She set out across the land and had no trouble finding the lair. Rallying her bravery and stilling her mind, Adira strode forth and tore down the barrier, ignoring the door completely.

The trolls jumped up in fright, hissing at the sunlight hitting the pale skin of their arms and legs. As they backed further into the shadows, she followed the retreat until she saw it: the glowing beacon from which they had been drawing their strength.

So she turned off the WiFi router and tore their precious fibre optic cable into shreds.

Coming Out

Talia stared into the mirror of her dressing table, hoping the reflection staring back would offer some clarity. But just like it never had any of the previous times she'd tried before, there was no luck today, either.

She clenched her fist and brought it down on the wooden surface, repressing a swear word. Today was when she really could have used that clarity more than ever before.

There was a knock, and her bedroom door opened a creak.

"Talia?" It was her father.

"I'm in here."

"Are you ready?"

She looked again at the mirror, her eyes pleading, but there was no change. Talia hung her head. "No."

"Talia?" Father asked again.

She shook her head, knowing she'd have to put her pity and doubt aside and just get on with it. A little louder she said, "I'm not ready. I'll be down in a minute."

"The coach is outside," said Father. "You've been getting dressed up all day."

Talia didn't know how to respond, so said nothing.

Father held the pause for a moment longer, then asked, "Are you decent?"

"Yes."

He pushed the door the rest of the way open and gasped.

Talia stood up and ran to the other side of the room. "Don't look at me!"

"But, Talia. You're a vision!"

"I'm not!" She wanted to scream. She'd been holding it in, all this time, and had thought she could keep holding until the whole stupid party was over, but it was like something had suddenly shifted, and it all came rushing out. She turned to face her father. "I'm a fraud!"

Father's face clouded in obvious confusion. He opened his mouth to ask something, or maybe offer more supposedly soothing words, but they seemed lost. And just as suddenly as all of Talia's frustration and anger at herself had frothed over, it was like a trap door opened in the pit of her stomach and it all emptied out again, leaving her empty. Weak.

Talia crumpled on the bed, her limbs automatically folding themselves into the foetal position. She cried, knowing it would ruin her make-up, but not caring. Everything was ruined anyway.

The mattress depressed to Talia's left, telling her that Father had sat down beside her, and then she felt his fingers—slow and deliberate—begin to stroke her hair, just like he had when she was young, or sick.

Talia sat up. "Daddy, am I sick?"

"Sweetie, no," he said, seemingly automatically, but then he paused, flustered. "I don't know what's wrong. Won't you tell me?"

How could she tell him? It was hard enough just trying to understand it herself.

"Is it about the party?" he prompted, and she nodded. She had to look down. Away. Anywhere but at the person dearest to her in the world, because just the thought of his disappointment was enough to tear her in two. She didn't think she could bear the reality of seeing it up close.

"Talia, this party is a good thing. It's for you and your friends to celebrate. Why has it got you all upset?"

"Because… because—" She hiccupped and shook her head again, hoping it would help reset her brain.

Her father's fingers left her hair and he took her hands in his, instead. "You know that no matter what you declare tonight, I love you. There's no shame, only acceptance."

She'd heard those words so many times, but they never quite rang true. Not with her. Not deep down. Because… Here it was, the truth she'd been trying to run away from, but could never quite escape. It was almost in step with her, so close now that letting it close the final inch felt inevitable. Like surrender. After everything, it was almost a relief.

Talia swallowed and her voice shook. "How can there be acceptance of nothing?" she asked, knowing there couldn't. Over all the years, she'd never yet heard of anyone who didn't fit *somewhere*.

Father's hands squeezed hers just a little tighter, until she looked up. "What do you mean?"

"I mean…" *Deep breath in, one, two.* Talia steadied her gaze. "Daddy, I don't have anything to declare. I don't know what—or who—I am."

Father frowned. It was a long time before he said anything, and Talia felt the slow death of the wait. Was he finally going to tell her she was wrong? That she didn't belong? Well, she already knew that, but hearing it would be worse. She held her breath, bracing herself.

"You're twenty-one now," Father said at last, surprising her.

"I am," she affirmed, no idea what his point was.

"When you didn't take part in a sixteenth coming-out party, your papa and I didn't worry. It wasn't all that uncommon."

Talia's skin flushed cold all over, the weight of his words sinking in. It had been five years. She'd not debuted at a seventeenth, eighteenth, nineteenth, or twentieth coming-out party either. This was her last shot, and he'd been so hoping she'd finally have her shit together. All she'd had to do was gain a little self-awareness, and she'd failed him.

"We figured it was probably better to wait," Father went on, "if you were unsure. Not that there's any shame in realising something more about yourself, later on, and coming out again, but it tends to be easier if you can pin it down the first time. We wanted things to be easy for you, your papa and I."

Tears stabbed at Talia's eyes. Why did he have to keep bringing up Papa? As much as grief had consumed her when they lost him—because losing a parent was always bound to consume you, especially if it's sudden—Talia had at least consoled herself that at least one of her dads would never have to live through her shame. But now, it was like Father was saying she was still letting him down, dead or not. She couldn't bear it. She tried to get up. To pace, or pack a bag. Maybe run down the hall and out to the carriage, telling the driver to take her anywhere.

But Father held on. Not so much that the grip hurt, just that she was anchored. Safe, despite everything. Talia was terrified to think of what would happen when he finally let go.

"Talia," said Father, her name infused with so much love it hurt. Was he hurting as much as she was? He had to be. "If you don't want to go to the party, you don't have to."

A gasp of shock escaped her. "But of course I do," she said automatically. "It's not just a party, it's a rite of passage. You know that. *Everyone* knows that."

"Sure," said Father. "But that puts a lot of pressure on it. On you. I don't want you to feel distressed. Today's about celebration, and acceptance."

There were those words again. They reached into Talia's chest, past her self-loathing, and tapped into a well of rage underneath.

"Everyone always says that!" she said, voice raised now. Words frantic. Talia hadn't known where to find them, but now here they were, unvarnished and ready to spew out at top speed. "Why does there have to be this big tradition? Can't I just be me? Whoever that is? Can't I just be left alone, as I am? As nothing?"

"Talia!" exclaimed Father, aghast. "You are not nothing!"

Finally, she wrenched her hands from him. "I'm not anything else! At least," she deflated, her lungs heaving for breath, "I don't think so. I don't feel gay, or straight, or pan, or any of the other categories. None of them fit right."

"Could—?" Father began to ask, but Talia held up a hand.

"I don't feel asexual or aromantic, either. There are feelings, they're just not…" she waved a hand, the descriptor as intangible as that which it was trying to describe.

"Talia," Father tried again, voice back to soothing. "This clearly matters to you. I'm sorry you felt the need to keep it all bottled up. You could have talked to me."

She looked at him, speechless, because they were finally talking, and it wasn't helping anything. Couldn't he see that?

"Listen," he said, "You really don't have to put yourself through this."

"No," she said, firm, because she'd thought that scenario through to its natural conclusion already. "Not having a coming out party would make me a freak, an outcast. It would be worse than just pretending to be something I'm not."

Father went to object, but she wouldn't hear it.

"I've made my peace," she said, resolutely.

"It doesn't sound like it."

"Well." She faltered a little, because okay, she had just freaked out about it all. He clearly wasn't wrong. "As much peace as I can," she amended.

Father shook his head. "No, I'm sorry, that's not good enough."

Her heart sank. She'd worked herself up into feeling halfway ready to be strong, but his declaration took the wind out of her. "Daddy," she pleaded, almost crying again.

He stood up. "You listen here, Talia Greenfield. I love you and am not going to let you settle for a label that doesn't fit, just to make other people more comfortable. I will accept nothing less than your complete comfort and total happiness. Well," he added, second-guessing that last part, "as happy as anyone can be, that is. Imperfect world and all."

Fresh tears slipped down Talia's face, but somewhere between gathering in her eyes and dripping off the end of her chin, they switched from liquid sadness into ones infused with happiness. Love.

Father opened his arms and Talia all but ran into them, letting him envelop her in a hug like she hadn't had in years, when Father and Papa would practically crush her between them and she'd revel in the safety of it.

There was a knock at the door, and a maid popped her head in to remind them the coach was waiting.

"Damn the coach!" exclaimed Father, making Talia laugh in surprise. She couldn't think of when she'd last seen him so animated. "Tell the driver he can—"

"Wait," said Talia, making him halt, mid-sentence, and stare at her. She swallowed. "He can wait. I just need to redo my make-up."

The maid nodded and backed out of the room, closing the door again.

"Talia?" asked Father. "We've been over this."

"I know," she said, "but it's okay. I still don't know what I'm going to tell the announcer, but I've got the coach ride to figure it out. I still have uncertainty, but I'm pretty sure I'll kick myself later if I miss out on the party."

Father smiled a little wryly, and she noticed his eyes were also damp. "You know, if you decided to never come out—or do it when you're sixty-five—it would be okay by me. I'd start a new tradition. Throw you the biggest party you've ever seen, and make it just for you."

Talia beamed back at him, her heart aching with how full it felt. "Thank you," she whispered, belatedly realising that yes, she most definitely should have brought all this up sooner. She approached her dressing table and got to work removing her streaked mascara and powder.

Father came to stand behind her, his hand resting on her shoulder. "Maybe you could just tell them you're undeclared," he mused aloud, but she shook her head.

"It doesn't really seem in the spirit of it," she said. "I'll think of something else." Mostly she was just glad to be rid of the feeling of guilt and wrongness eating at her from the inside out. What she told the announcer to declare her as barely mattered, compared to the weight off her shoulders.

Still at her shoulder, she saw the reflection of Father's face draw back into a frown, and she paused, make-up wipe halfway down her face and heart in her mouth. What had he realised? What on earth was he going to say now, sure to set her spinning again?

"Talia," he began, tentatively.

"Yes?" She sighed at the shake that had re-entered her voice.

"Clearly you've been thinking about all this a long time—and I heard you when you said you'd considered each of the labels and not settled on one. I don't want you to think I'm doubting you, but—"

"Spit it out," she said, because beating around the bush was only making things harder again.

"Well," said Father, "have you thought about Questioning?"

She turned to him, her brow feeling pinched between her eyebrows. "What do you mean? I've been questioning this whole time. Isn't that what we've been talking about? What I've—"

Father raised his hands in a 'hold on' motion, and she stopped.

"I mean, as a label. As your declaration." He chuckled, but it sounded like anything but easy laughter. "You could just come out as just that. As Questioning."

Talia thought about that for what felt like a long time. Because, truth was, this wasn't in fact one of the possibilities she'd considered. "Isn't 'questioning' just something someone is before they figure out what they actually are, and *then* come out?"

Father shrugged. "Doesn't have to be."

Talia felt her frown deepen. "I... I don't know. It kind of feels like cheating. Like just as bad as undeclared."

Father shook his head. "There is no bad. No wrong way to be a human, Talia. Labels are made to serve us, not the other way around. Part of the freedom to declare yourself anything you want is to make the definition your own. You've just said that you've been questioning this whole time, so maybe..." He trailed off, but she picked up the thought, warming to it.

"Maybe I just need to accept that," she said, feeling the epiphany of it the moment the words left her lips. *This is only a pressure-filled nightmare if I let it be. I could be anything, can embrace uncertainty as a part of myself and let it be, the way I wanted everyone else to leave it alone. God, why hadn't I seen that before?*

Probably because I hadn't let anyone in to talk about it before, she belatedly realised.

"Thank you," she told Father again, and he gave her his best smile.

"You really do look a vision," he said. "Especially now, with an extra light in your eyes."

Talia released a deep breath and stood up, feeling all the way unburdened. Finally feeling ready. She let her father take her hand and guide her towards the door.

"And you know," he whispered in her ear, as he helped her into the coach, "I wasn't kidding about throwing you another party, later. No matter the age, or the declaration."

Talia laughed. It might take another five years—or ten, or twenty, but it didn't matter. It was the freedom of the option.

"I'll think about it," she said at last.

"Take all the time you need," said Father.

Robin

Blonde-haired, blue-eyed, and perfectly playing the role of the charming ditz, Robin made her way through the swarming club, apologising sweetly and laughing a little to herself each time she bumped into a different guy.

The men always took her clumsy nature with great grace. It was a credit to each of them.

To Robin, each of them was a credit card or a set of keys.

As she entered the back office and sat down opposite John and Mary Little, she couldn't help but roll her eyes at the guys' combined stupidity as she emptied her pockets onto the huge desk before pulling off her wig and taking out her contact lenses. The left one always stuck.

"How was it today?" asked Mary.

"Too easy," said Robin, "None of them recognized me at all."

John smiled as he counted the money. "Serves them right then, doesn't it?" he said, before releasing a deep, rolling belly laugh.

The children at the orphanage would eat well tonight.

The Locksmith

Jamelia was worried. For the most part, she thought of herself as a Strong Independent Woman, and she liked the feel of that thought. But sometimes, like now, she wished she was more of a Strong Semi-Independent Woman who had at least a small support network she could trust.

Crime rates in her area had gone through the roof over the course of a month and were still gathering speed. It had been burglaries and trespassing, mostly, but the police couldn't figure out why. Some people had been caught in the act and arrested, but still the crimes carried on. Eventually it had been realised that there was no single group or gang carrying them out. In fact, there was only one thing that linked all of the crimes, and that was the lack of evidence pointing to forced entry.

Under interrogation, the police were told that houses and businesses had been left open, that word had got around and criminals just started trying their luck, testing door handles at random. Word spread further, tempting new people to crime, and the practice increased. The affected house and shop owners were insistent that they closed up just as usual, however, and the police wondered if there was a conspiracy to claim insurance money going on.

All of that played on Jamelia's mind, but none of it bothered her so much as the fact that, for the last three mornings, she'd come downstairs to find her own front door without the lock on, house open to the world—and she lived alone.

No one had come in or done anything, as far as she could tell, but that only made it weirder in her book. According to the police, there was no room for her details in *their* book. They said it wasn't a crime, yet, and they were too busy trying to keep up with ones that had already happened.

The deep sense of vulnerability—of fragility—Jamelia had felt since her sister's death the year before became all the more acute at the lack of response. At having reached for help only to have been denied.

She sincerely wished she didn't live alone anymore, but it didn't exactly feel like a good time to start inviting strangers to move in, and who else did she have?

Jamelia could get a dog, maybe. As both a companion and guard.

While she mulled that option over, she bought three new locks—a second one for her front door, one for an interior door that led from her living room to the stairs and landing, and one for her bedroom door, right at the top. The man in the shop said she was lucky to get them, that they were the last of his stock, but Jamelia did not feel lucky.

The first two nights after finding her door open, she had barely slept as she tried to keep guard, but it hadn't made any difference—she'd made sure no one had been in her room, sure, but somehow that front door of hers had still gotten unlocked and she hadn't seen a damn thing she could tell police about it.

Not that she trusted them to do much at that point, anyway. She was just a silly woman wasting their time. A single woman, alone in the big bad world probably looking for attention amidst the chaos.

On the third night of her watch, tiredness had gotten the better of Jamelia and she'd slept soundly the whole night through. But waking up to yet again find her door open had been the final straw.

News reporters on breakfast TV discussed the phenomenon with experts who theorised that mass hysteria was making the general public forgetful. Jamelia almost convinced herself that this was the case and took extra care to double and triple-check she'd bolted all three doors on her way to bed, the fourth night.

She slept fitfully for the first part, finally falling into a deeper sleep and dreams of her sister, only to be woken by a noise. After sitting up and listening out for a moment, she told herself her mind was playing tricks. She'd only just got back to sleep when the noise came again, louder.

Jamelia jumped up and looked out her window, but could see nothing. She considered calling the police but feared more dismissal. Maybe even an official caution for wasting their time.

Turning to her bedroom door, she discovered that finding an open lock was not that scary—not when you compared it to opening an unlocked door, and finding someone staring back at you. And oh, didn't she wish to be alone now?

Wingman

Lorna should have trusted her instincts and just stayed home. But Grey was always so persuasive, damn him.

"Come on," he'd said, "it'll be fun. A night out on the tiles is just what you need to forget about bitch-face."

For a second, Lorna had believed it might be possible. Grey had seized on her hesitation, and now here she was, staring at the bathroom tiles of some fabulous club she couldn't remember the name of, regretting the whole thing.

With a groan, Lorna lifted her head from between her knees and stood up. She could do this. All it would take was stepping back into the thumping music and telling Grey she'd had enough. She could be back home and in her pyjamas in under an hour, if the traffic worked in her favour. But when was the last time anything had worked in her favour?

She braced herself, opened the cubicle door, and narrowly missed colliding with a hot blonde who'd been, she assumed, looking for an empty stall.

"Shit!" they said in unison, before sharing a brief smile.

Lorna could have sworn there was a spark between them, but before she opened her mouth to ask for a name, let alone a number, the hot blonde blushed and ducked her head.

"If I could, um…." She gestured to the toilet door that Lorna was still blocking. "I mean, you're done, right?"

"Er, right," murmured Lorna, face flushing as she stepped out of her way. As soon as the door was closed, she considered banging her head against it. Because, *god! What kind of idiot am I? Making moon-eyes at some chick just wanting to pee in private.* She shook her head, braced herself, and exited the bathroom back into the club proper.

Thankfully, it wasn't hard to find Grey. It never was. Wherever he happened to be, there was sure to be a crowd all around him. Sometimes an honest-to-god spotlight, too. Like he was the superstar he believed himself to be, or some random computer character with a side-quest.

Lorna was trying to figure out how to navigate her way through the crowd when Grey caught sight of her and made his way over, the crowd splitting for him like the Red Sea.

"There you are!" He air-kissed her cheek. "Where have you been?"

"Hiding?" she hedged. "Making a tit of myself?"

"Oh, Lorn!" He squeezed her hand sympathetically and pouted. Actually pouted, as if he were a sixteen-year-old schoolgirl. "Not having fun?"

Lorna sighed, knowing she couldn't resist the pout, no matter how ridiculous it was. "I'm just not feeling it."

"But Lorn!" exclaimed Grey, batting his eyelashes, which were infuriatingly longer, and darker, and curlier than she could ever get hers. "I need you to be my wingman. There's this gorgeous blonde floating about who is to die for!"

Lorna frowned. "You want me to try and chat her up for you? Why?" God knows he didn't need the help. Was this just another pity thing to make her feel included?

"Please?" he said, batting his eyelashes again.

Bloody hell. "If I do this, will you please just let me go home?"

Grey opened his mouth—probably to talk her into not only doing what he wanted, but staying to watch *and* something else on the side, just because he could—when his eyes suddenly glittered.

Lorna turned to see what he was looking at and made eye contact with the blonde from the bathroom again.

"There she is!" said Grey, delighted.

Well, damn. "Fine, I'll go talk to her. But that's all, right?" Lorna moved off before he could answer. It was best to just get it over with.

An apology seemed as good of an opener as anything else, so she started there. "Uh, hi. I wanted to say sorry about before."

The blonde smiled and—*gah!*—it was dazzling. "Are you sorry for the weirdness or the almost concussion?"

Lorna bit her lip. "Uh, both, I guess? Anyway, I'm sorry. My name's Lorna, by the way."

The blonde put out her hand. "Shannon."

As inconspicuously as she could, which was probably as obvious as all hell, Lorna rubbed her sweaty palm on her jeans and shook the offered hand. "Nice to meet you, Shannon." It still felt as weird as before, standing there, trying to be cool while at the same time both trying to show a little interest and figure out if there was any interest going the other way.

To try and limit her mortification at least a little, Lorna shoved all her thoughts aside and just got on with it. It didn't matter that she was interested, because (a) she was a freak, (b) she was on a mission, and (c) Shannon was probably straight. The super cute ones always were.

"Listen, I know this is weird, but you see my friend over there?"

Shannon followed her gaze and nodded. "The life and soul of the party? Sure. What about him?"

"That's my friend Grey. He likes you, and it would be doing me a really big favour if you would go over and talk to him." Lorna was going to add a casual "no pressure" at the end of her spiel, but Shannon had nodded again and was already off. *Typical.*

Lorna idled on the edge of the dance floor, watching as Grey and Shannon laughed and whispered in each other's ears. She wondered how long should she give it before she could officially consider herself off the clock and leave without feeling absentee best friend guilt, but then Shannon looked up at her and smiled again. *Damn it all.*

Lorna hoped to god Grey wasn't talking about her. He was always saying something, and it was rarely good. Like oh, for example, dragging her out tonight when he wasn't going to actually spend that much time with her.

Although she had to admit that, as Grey had promised, she hadn't thought about

Ashton once. (Or bitch-face, as Grey liked to call her.) Maybe the night had been good for something after all.

Regardless, Lorna made her way to the bar at the same time she saw Grey heading there. She'd done what he'd asked, and now she was definitely going home. She'd opened her mouth to tell him just that when he announced, "You are the worst wingman ever!"

Lorna reared back, offended on top of everything else. "Excuse me?"

Grey shook his head. "You only sent me over a lesbian."

Lorna's mouth hung open. "What? You— I mean, you specifically asked for—"

"It's okay," Grey continued, as if she hadn't spoken, "because *she* is a good wingman." He leaned close and added in a whisper, "Shannon tells me the barman's been checking me out all night. I'm gonna go for it."

Lorna blinked at him. "Shannon's a lesbian?"

"Oh, totally," said Grey, complete with dismissive hand wave. "She's totally into you, by the way."

"She— What?" No, that couldn't be right. Could it?

Grey gave her a little nudge. "Go on. She's waiting for you to talk to her again. Honestly, Lorn, do I have to do all the work?"

After another long look at her best friend to make sure he was serious, Lorna laughed. "You did this on purpose, didn't you?"

He winked but denied all knowledge.

Lorna shook her head but kissed him on the cheek. Grey might be utterly ridiculous in many ways, but she had to admit he had real wingman skills of his own.

Caretaker

My mum hasn't been right in a long time. I'd never say it out loud, but I'm not sure if she ever was. It's been getting worse, though, since we lost Dad.

The thing is that her parents spoiled her in the very literal sense. As in, they indulged her so much, she never grew up or had a hard day in her life that someone didn't come along and fix for her.

So, when they died, she broke. I can't imagine what it must have been like to go from having zero problems to having to deal with maybe the hardest thing in the world. If my dad hadn't been there to pick her up and keep her going, I don't think she'd have made it. And that's not an exaggeration. She doesn't know how to take care of herself. Like, at all.

Such people really shouldn't have kids, in my opinion, but she was happy with my dad, and he always said that I came along as a natural extension of that happiness.

My dad was seriously the sweetest guy. It hurts just thinking about him. It hurts my mum so much, it's like he's blanked from her memory. She walks around in a daze, talking and giggling to herself.

Sometimes, I'm not sure she even knows who I am.

She fights me as I try to get her dressed, or give her breakfast, and she won't look at the baby at all. It's like she's regressed right back to his level, and anything other than sleep or play is too hard, too bright and violent.

I've been so busy dealing with everything, I almost forgot about Christmas. At first, I thought my mum had forgotten, too, but then it dawned on me—she'd started chattering about Santa, almost chanting his name some nights in her sleep.

It wasn't that she'd *forgotten* to buy gifts or organise anything, I realised. In her broken little baby brain, she'd convinced herself that Saint Nick is coming along to make everything right.

The knife in my gut twists that little bit more every time I think about it. It's just so hard to believe that she used to be a clever, articulate woman who, despite not having the barest thread of self-reliance, was bright and vivacious.

Don't read this and think for a second that she couldn't understand love or that my dad took advantage. When they first met, as kids, it was her who chased him. They went to the same prep school, and he didn't want to date her at first, because she always scored higher than him on tests. But he always loved her; that's what he told me.

My dad told me to take care of her. When I think back to that last conversation we had, I can almost convince myself that he knew he was going to get hit by a truck, and that my mum would snap once and for all.

I'm trying to be strong—really, I am––but it's so hard, and I know I can't last much longer.

When I slept in too long the other day, Mum tried to light the fire, and the whole house almost went up. Every moment with her is so dangerous, and I can't risk taking my eyes off the baby at all. I know she's ignoring him now, but what if she flips again and does something we really can't come back from?

It doesn't bear thinking about. So I'm here, keeping things together. At least until Christmas.

I got all these presents with the last of Dad's savings, and have been cooking for a week. Mum is going to be so stoked when she sees what "Santa" has got her.

In the New Year, I'll call social services and it will all come crashing down. But, until then, I think I can make the magic just about stretch to fit the days.

Nightmares in Bliss

"I spy with my little eye…"

"Do we have to play this?"

"…something beginning with M."

"You're just gonna ignore me, then? What if I play the silence game instead of your stupid—"

"It's a mouse."

"What?"

"A mouse."

"Where? No, don't just shrug at me! Are you serious? Macie, if there is a mouse I'm gonna scream, I swear."

"Relax."

"Oh, you relax! Were you making that up?"

"Maybe."

"I can't believe you! All your stupid games and pranks. Why did you bring me up here, anyway? I'm cold."

"Here."

"No, I don't want your jacket. Take me home."

"Look, I'm sorry, okay? I was just trying to lighten the mood. Take the coat, please."

"Well, okay. But you have to tell me why we're here. It looks like it's going to rain, and we're miles from anywhere."

"This is where it started."

"Here we go. Where what started?"

"Us."

"Mace—"

"Okay, okay, hear me out."

"Fine. What is it?"

"This, my darling, is the place I was sitting when I first saw your face."

"Here?"

"Yep."

"Really?"

"Yeah."

"Why?"

"I'd run away. This is always where I came."

"But there's nothing here. It looks like even the usual trash you'd find on a beach has got up and left. How did you even get a WiFi signal?"

"I was tethering."

"That doesn't make any sense. You came to a barren beach to tether internet, just so you could scroll through dating profiles? What happened to running away?"

"Jen."

"What?"

"You're missing the point."

"Only because you keep beating around the bush. Oh, would you look at that, you actually managed to find a single landmark in this deserted, barren, cold-ass beach.

Congratulations, you have a bush to beat around."

"I'm building up to something here."

"Fine. Okay. Beat around, build, or do whatever else it is you're planning, just get to the—"

"Look, I'm trying to propose, but if you don't quit bitching I'm never gonna be able to—"

"You what?"

"Stop interrupting me!"

"Wait, no. Hang on."

"You hang on, Jen. This was supposed to be romantic."

"Say that thing again."

"What thing? When I called you a bitch?"

"No, you idiot. The other thing."

"The… Oh, crap. I said it."

"Mace…"

"Yeah?"

"Is there something you want to ask me?"

"Eh, well… I've kind of ruined it now, haven't I?"

"Nope. Doesn't matter. I officially don't care. This is the most romantic place ever."

"Really? I mean, it is quite bleak."

"No. It's perfect, honestly. Do it."

"Here?"

"Yeah."

"Now?"

"Yes! Oh my god, get on with it. You're such a tease!"

"I am, aren't I?"

"Mace!"

"Right, okay. Here goes."

"What's that?"

"My speech."

"You have a speech?"

"Of course."

"All written out like that? It seems short."

"Are you gonna let me do this or not?"

"Sorry. Yes. Wow me."

"Okay, okay. Right, I can do this. Jen. Uh, Jennifer. You…you're a nightmare, but I love you. Do you wanna make it official and–
–"

"You really are shocking at this."

"Yeah, well, you put me off!"

"Sorry. You forgive me?"

"I guess."

"Still wanna marry this nightmare?"

"Definitely."

"Okay then."

"Really? Just like that?"

"Sure. I mean, you're a nightmare too. But you're *my* nightmare."

"I'm totally putting that in the vows."

"If you do, I'm dragging you back here for wedding photographs."

"Drag me here for wedding photographs, and I'm totally gonna be the one behind the camera. In the car. About a mile down the road where there's central heating."

"It is quite nippy, isn't it?"

"Yes, now come on. We have a disaster to plan."

"Be still, my beating heart."

Tangled

Rick pulled into his driveway, turned off the engine, and rested his head on the steering wheel of his Jeep. His day had started off badly, and the long hours at work didn't help. He'd been dreading coming home, knowing he'd have to finally start an uncomfortable conversation with his housemate, Christopher, but it just couldn't be put off any longer. Well, not more than a few minutes, anyway—long enough to roll down the window and have a cigarette.

The smoking was a bad sign; even Rick himself knew that. He'd managed to give up for six months before the stress of the morning pushed him back.

Susan had been there, at the house, standing in the middle of the rose bed of all places, near where the front wheel of the Jeep had now come to rest. Thorns had cut her bare legs and feet, so she had trickles and smears of blood all over.

Rick's face had fallen when he saw her—he felt pity for her, at first—but then he got angry when she wouldn't go. So now he had to have the talk with Christopher, and they'd have to decide what to do about her because enough was enough.

"Christopher, we have to talk," Rick repeated over to himself before shaking his head. No. It was a bad opener. 'Did you see Susan this morning?' he could ask, but that was maybe too direct.

Raising his eyes from the cigarette, Rick surveyed the house. There didn't seem to be any lights on. Maybe he could go in and shower before having to decide anything. Except that was a cop-out. It was better for him to be prepared. That much was clear when he'd found Susan with wild hair and wearing only an oversized T-shirt at seven am.

Rick hadn't known what to say. She had looked like she might cry, so they had just stood there for a minute looking at each other until a neighbour came out to collect the milk and Rick had tried to get Susan to move further into the shade where she wouldn't cause a scene.

Fat lot of good that had done him.

Susan had wrenched her arm from his hand and started to yell and swear at him. Rick had backed up and raised his hands in surrender, but he was firm about telling her she needed to go, that she shouldn't be there. And then she'd started up again about how she and Christopher were together, that she loved him, and needed him, that he knew she was there and didn't mind.

That was when Rick lost it and started yelling back at her that she was a stupid, deluded cow, and how if she cared about Christopher at all she wouldn't be putting him through this stalker bullshit.

She really did cry, then, and he felt like the biggest jerk on the planet. She was clearly mentally unstable. He and Christopher would probably have to notify the authorities and get her forcibly sectioned; get a restraining order, or something.

Rick flinched as ash from his cigarette fell onto his jeans and started to smoulder. He brushed his hand quickly over the patch to extinguish it and inspected the hole. It wasn't big, but was enough to be the crappy topping on his craptastic day. He opened the door, threw down what was left of the butt and swung his legs out of the car to stamp on it.

Each of the smaller actions that made up the bigger action of walking to the front door—rolling up the car window, closing the car door and locking it, and putting one foot in front of the other—sent mental exhaustion deeper into Rick's bones.

He had seen documentaries about asylums and didn't want to be responsible for anyone being locked up in one. Sure, they probably weren't as bad as they'd been in the Victorian era—he was pretty sure they weren't even called asylums anymore—but there had been a thing in the newspaper the other week about how vulnerable adults were more likely to be abused when put into care or some shit. He didn't want that on his conscience.

Susan used to be a really cool person before her obsession with Christopher started and her friendship with both him and Rick went to hell. Rick and Christopher had been best friends since primary school, and Susan had been the one to plant the roses for them. They were a housewarming gift for when they'd moved in together right after uni. Except neither of them had really cared to learn how to look after roses, so they were kinda wild.

Truth be told, Rick had fallen hard for Susan that very first day he saw her walking across campus with a huge smile on her face. He'd turned and asked Christopher what he thought, but he'd only grunted.

Christopher hadn't really ever shown any interest. Not only did he refuse to acknowledge any of Susan's weird appearances at their house, he'd tried to talk Rick out of asking her out in the first place.

Two weeks into knowing Susan, Rick had been talking Christopher's ear off about how much he liked her—again—and had again asked his friend's opinion. This time, different from the rest for whatever reason, Christopher had shaken his head and actually engaged with the topic at hand.

"I don't think so," he'd said. "She's nuts."

Rick had gotten indignant and asked exactly what he meant, and Christopher had shrugged and just said it was obvious. Rick thought he was being a prick at the time but now, well, look who turned out to be right. That same day, Rick had gone to Susan's flat and asked her out regardless of what his friend thought. She'd been really sweet about it and said she was flattered but, ultimately, told him she was already with someone else.

And that's when the lies about Christopher started. Susan said they'd been dating for "a while" but he'd wanted to keep it quiet. Briefly Rick had wondered if it might be true, but that didn't make any sense. Christopher was already dating, like, three other girls, and—now Rick thought about it––he'd never really had a kind word to say about Susan. Maybe, he realised belatedly, this was why. Given what each of them had told him, he figured she'd tried it on, he'd rejected her, and she hadn't taken it well so was now in some deluded fantasy land of her own making.

It wasn't the first time something like that had happened. Christopher seemed to have all kinds of women coming out of the woodwork—especially the crazy ones— while Rick struggled to ever find a date. He sighed, considering again that was maybe for the best. "Better no girl than a crazy one," Christopher always told him. And sure, wasn't he one to know?

Rick figured it must be really hard on his friend to have to put up with stalkers. He assumed he felt sorry for the women, and was just putting on the callous act as some kind of coping mechanism. Whatever it was, it had to stop. Christopher needed to talk to Rick about this, and they needed to do something, because this was worse than any of the times before and Susan needed to be made to stay away before she did something really bad that she couldn't come back from.

Resolute, Rick put his key in the front door and walked into the house, flicking on the hall switch and effectively flooding the whole open-plan downstairs area with light.

Christopher and Susan looked up, surprise on their faces.

Susan was naked, backed up against the sink, Christopher standing between her parted legs, his bare chest pressed to hers and mouth smeared with her lipstick.

They both looked away as suddenly as they had looked up.

Rick dropped his keys and swore, bending to pick them up. By the time he had righted himself and remembered to breathe, Christopher had disentangled himself from the embrace and walked the short distance to his bedroom, shutting the door loudly behind him—not saying a word or tossing any kind of backward glance towards Susan, whom he'd left standing there, exposed and adrift.

All the scars on her legs were vibrant red.

Rick blinked after his friend and Susan burst into tears. He had to dig out an oversized shirt from the recesses of his wardrobe for her to wear and make her a cup of tea before either of them were composed enough for him to offer a lift home.

Christopher's bedroom door was locked and, apparently, all of Susan's clothes were on his floor. Rick seethed as reality filtered through the sludge of his overworked mind.

"How long?" he asked, when he finally found his voice.

"Four months," said Susan, her head down and voice shaky.

"Right," said Rick, clenching and unclenching his fist. He *definitely* needed to have a serious talk with his housemate now.

Because, of the three of them, there was definitely one liar and one deluded idiot; it just so happened that he'd got all the roles tangled.

Day Trip Trick

I knew it was a trap right away.

My teacher calls me a clever clogs, but always gets this look when she says it, so I know she doesn't really think that. But today I was clever for real. My mums thought I wouldn't figure it out, but I did, and I'm going to tell on them.

Well, as soon as I figure out who you're supposed to tell, anyway.

I always go to Mum when someone's mean, or teasing, but who do you call when they're the one trying to trick you? I think maybe the Ghostbusters, but I don't know their number, and I'm not supposed to use the phone.

"We've got a surprise for you," they said.

I stopped playing and looked up at them. "A surprise?"

"Yeah," they said, and they were smiling, which totally made it obvious. My mummies aren't very good at doing tricks, but I'm not going to tell them that. I just sat and watched them, waiting to see if I could figure out what was happening.

"Your aunt Alice is going to take you to the zoo today, and then you're going to go 'round to hers for lunch, and maybe ice cream."

I nodded and said, "Okay," because I'm better than them at being secret. I didn't want them to know that I knew there was something I didn't know.

When Alice came to pick me up, she was smiling too, so I knew I had to be on the lookout and get evidence for when I found a way to tell the Ghostbusters there was something wrong. I'd give them the clues and they could fix it so the adults aren't weird anymore.

All day, Alice was really nice. She didn't tell me off once—not even when I tried to get into the monkey cage. That gave me an idea, so I decided to be as bad as I could just to see how big of a trick it was.

I climbed a fence, and fell off a wall, and tried to feed a fruit pastel to a penguin, but Alice still was smiling, even if her teeth were all clenched behind her wide lips.

When the day was almost over, and I was eating my ice cream, I heard her say to uncle John that she didn't know why my mummies wanted "another one," when I was like this. I didn't know what she meant, and I don't think she thought I was listening, but I was and I think it must have been a very big clue, so I decided to tell the Ghostbusters that one first.

Finally, we got home. I was bored of the trick, so I decided to ask right away how to call the Ghostbusters—I thought maybe they don't have a phone, but a bat signal or something—but when I opened the door and opened my mouth to see what my mummies would say, I was distracted.

They were standing there, holding another baby.

I walked back out the door and around the side to Auntie Alice's car. She'd lost her smile, but tried to put it back on really quick when she saw me. It was too late, though, and she knew it. So she sighed and went back to being normal.

"Are you okay?" she asked me.

I shook my head. "I've decided I don't want to go in," I said. "Can I live with you, or at the zoo instead?"

That made the smile pop onto her face again, but it was different now. It made her cheeks go pink.

"No," she said, "You need to go in and meet your baby brother."

I sighed then too, and rolled my eyes. Adults hate it when you do that, but they do it all the time, so I think it's a silly rule and don't listen to it.

"Fine," I said, "but if he stays, I want more ice cream."

Dynamics

It was a bank holiday Monday, and Millie had zero plans. With the day off work, she figured she'd sleep in, take her time over the breakfast she usually didn't have time for at all, and then maybe bring her duvet to the sofa and binge-watch... something. She didn't much care what, so long as it required exactly zero brain power.

All of that had been well and good, going to plan as much as a no-plan day could go, and then she'd fallen asleep over a lazy Pot Noodle lunch, and woken up when the sky outside was starting to darken to the sound of someone knocking.

Millie blinked, at first not sure where she was or why. Having always been a heavy sleeper, the sensation of utter confusion upon returning to consciousness was far from new, and yet she never got used to it. Or at least never remembered that this always happened while it was in the middle of happening.

Someone knocked again, and Millie got to her feet on autopilot. She stumbled over to the outer door—the single entry and exit to her one-bedroom flat—trying her best to jump-start her brain as she shook out her hand, which she must have slept awkwardly on given the giant ball of pins and needles it had become.

A third knock.

"All right, all right, I'm com—" She swung open the door without thinking to check the peephole first, the rest of her complaint dying in her throat at who she saw. She hadn't really had any expectations for who it might be, but she certainly didn't expect—

"Max?"

He flinched under her gaze, tried for a smile, and gave up the attempt, instead casting his eyes to the side, very much looking like he might bolt.

Millie reached out with her dead arm in a feeble attempt to ward off such an outcome. "Are you okay?"

The second she said it, she realised how stupid it sounded. Because here he was, her estranged older brother, standing on her doorstep looking like absolute shite. He'd grown out his hair into a tangled, greasy nest, had bloodshot eyes, and a bruise on his right cheek. Okay was at least three postcodes from where he stood.

"I'm sorry," he told the ground at her feet. "I shouldn't have just… I—" He looked ready to run away again, which was honestly the most terrifying part of all. Because this was Max, quite possibly the most confident person Millie had ever met. Or at least he had been.

"It's okay," Millie found herself saying. *Why do I keep using that word? Nothing about this is fucking okay!* "Come in."

He looked up, meeting her eyes briefly before cringing away again. "Are you sure? I mean, I can—"

"Maxwell, get the hell in here so I can find out what's wrong!" ordered Millie, doing the best impression of Suzanne she could muster. Suzanne was their other sibling—Max's twin—and she had a way of telling people what to do that they somehow didn't mind following. Millie had never understood it, had never gotten any of her attempts to replicate it to work, and now realised—as Max burst into tears right there in front of her—that it was absolutely the wrong move to have made.

Jesus fuck, what had happened?
"Max."

He visibly fought to speak through the sobs thundering through him, making his thin frame shake. "D-don't call me that," he managed at last

What the hell? "O-okay. You should still come in. Please?"

Something like relief swirled in Millie as Max bobbed his head and allowed her to lead him to her kitchen nook, where she was swift in putting the kettle on to boil. *Mum always said a cup of tea solves everything, and God knows she had to be right about something eventually.*

"So," said Millie, after the prolonged silence in which she finished making the tea and had settled herself and Max on the too-small sofa. It was supposed to be a two-seater, but could only comfortably fit one and a half people, and only if they really liked each other.

Millie studied her brother's face, searching for some shred of a reason for why he was there, but drawing nothing but blanks. Because no, he'd never liked her. Or at least Max had thrown his lot in with Suzanne and their parents in their collective dislike of her. At any rate, there was probably more Millie should have added to her sentence, but she honestly couldn't think what.

Thankfully, it was enough to prompt Max anyway.

He sniffled and wrapped his hands more tightly around his mug. "I'm guessing you didn't hear from Mum."

Millie frowned at him. Because no, she hadn't. But of course she hadn't. Not hearing from their mother, or father,

Suzanne, or even Max for that matter had been the key part in Millie's whole 'cut the bastards out of your life so you never have to deal with their toxic shit ever again' plan. Either Max read this in her face, or engaged his brain and remembered it for himself, because he shook his head the next minute.

"Sorry. Stupid question. I just thought…" He shrugged, abandoning the sentence.

"Max," said Millie, realising the faux pas a moment too late. "Sorry, sorry!" Her brain flooded with panic hormones at the pained expression crossing her brother's face. "I didn't—I mean, is there a reason I shouldn't call you… *that name*? A-and is there something else I should call you instead?"

"I…" His mouth twisted to the side and he set down his mug, hands shaking again. "I haven't come up with anything yet. Or nothing I'm sure about."

Millie frowned at him. "Right, so…" She took a breath. "Okay, I'm gonna stick with 'hey you' for the time being, cool?"

A smile fluttered at the outer edge of his lips for a moment, and Millie's heart felt a little uplifted at the sight, but then he rocked forward, his elbows going to his knees and head in his hands as huge, wracking sobs took him a second time.

Fresh terror struck Millie at the sight. At the sound—how loud the crying was. She was worried her downstairs neighbour might actually call the police, and thought maybe they should. Tentatively she reached out a hand and ran it along her brother's back in what she hoped were soothing motions.

He turned his head to look at her through his mass of fringe and tear-stained eyes. "Why are you being nice to me?"

She blinked at the question, not sure how to answer. Wasn't it obvious? Millie wondered how you could witness someone in obvious distress and be anything *but* nice to them… but then she was reminded again of their mother.

"I've been a shit," he continued, sniffling.

Millie got up and retrieved a box of tissues from her bedroom and handed them over. She had needed the few moments the action took in order to think. "Yes," she said now. "You have."

"I'm sorry," he said, wiping his eyes. "Millie, I'm—"

Before he crumbled into more weeping, she sat down again and took firm hold of the hand he wasn't using to blow his nose. His fingernails were filthy.

"It's done," said Millie. "If you're really sorry, you can show me by not treating me that way again." She swallowed, because part of her had always wanted to say that—or be in a position to say something like it, but she'd never pictured it being like this. "In the meantime, I need you to tell me what the fuck happened. Are you…" Her brain shuffled through a bunch of possibilities, but none of them seemed to fit with what she knew of her brother. *Addicted to something? On the run from the police? A boyfriend?*

"I'm trans, Millie."

"Oh." All of her thoughts stopped. *"Ohhh. That…" Trans? Okay, didn't see that coming, but why is he—urgh,* she. *They?—acting like it's the end of the world?*

"Mum and Dad kicked me out."

"Well, fuck." *That would do it.*

"Yeah."

"Are… Millie, are you gonna—?"

"What?"

"If you want me to go, just say. You don't need to yell, or anything, I'll just…"

The words, "Fuck off!" exploded from Millie without her knowing in advance they were coming. "You think I'd kick you out? Come here." She wrapped her arms around them in what was almost more of a stranglehold than a hug before realising they might not actually be comfortable with the contact and releasing them again. "Sorry."

For what had to be at least the sixth time in the space of an hour, tears filled their eyes, but they looked different now. They reached for Millie and held her back just as fiercely.

The two of them sat like that for a while, then Millie got another dead arm and decided it was a sign from the universe they needed more tea. "I'd offer you something stronger, but all I've got is…" She looked through her cupboard. "Harveys Bristol Cream."

"What the fuck is that?"

"A kind of sherry, I think."

"Sherry?"

Millie shrugged. "Someone left it here after a house party. It's pretty rank."

They decided to stick with tea. And the rest of the story came out. How the person formerly known as Max had come to realise they didn't feel like the person everyone thought they were. How they'd thought it was safe to tell Suzanne, because they'd always been close, and everyone had taken it well enough when Max had initially thought he was gay.

But Suzanne flipped out. She blurted it to their parents before they'd been ready, and Max had been told to leave. Then after they left, in the car their parents had bought them for their seventeenth birthday four years ago, their dad had taken the extra step of reporting it stolen. From there, there had been an arrest, a caution, and two weeks of bouncing between homeless shelters that weren't set up to 'handle' someone like that.

"Fucking hell." Millie regretted not opening the sherry.

"Yeah," they said again, their voice so small. So... broken.

God, Millie could strangle their mum, dad, and Suzanne too. What the fuck made them think they could treat someone like that? Millie shook her head, realising it was probably the same thing that had compelled her parents to make her the butt of all their jokes and nasty comments for the unforgivable crime of never fitting in as she grew up. Not being the pretty one like Suzanne, or the smart one like Max. But she couldn't think about that now, had to push it down and deal with the more pressing issue that had landed in her lap.

"Listen," said Millie. "You can stay here. For as long as you like. There's only one bedroom, but I've got the sofa here, and––What? Why are you looking at me like that?"

"Are you serious? Y-you mean that?"

"Yes," said Millie, kind of impressed at the amount of defiance in her own voice.

"Millie, I don't know if…" They trailed off, probably remembering their lack of other options.

"It'll be okay," said Millie. "Maybe not super long term, but until you get back on your feet. We'll figure it out."

They shook their head. "I still don't get it. How you of all people are so… nice."

Millie raised an eyebrow in what she hoped was a devil-may-care kind of way. "I'm gonna not take that as an insult."

"God, you know what I mean."

She smiled a little. "Yeah, I do."

"You're actually pretty great, you know."

Millie laughed and said, "I'll take it." She wished she could keep the conversation in the lighter tone it had shifted to, but knew that instinct was just fear talking. "Listen," she said again, pushing through the discomfort. "I know you said that you hadn't settled on a name, and I get that, but I'm not sure 'hey you' is actually gonna work. Have you, um…" Millie bit the inside of her cheek. "Did you settle on any pronouns?"

"Yeah." Their face actually lit up a little. "I'm okay with they, but she/her, mostly."

Millie nodded once. "Okay."

"And you know," continued her sister, nervously shredding a tissue between her fingers, "I had been thinking of a name. I'm just not sure if it's stupid."

"Okay," repeated Millie. "Hit me."

Her sister blushed a little then said, "Angelica?" They posed it like a question.

"You mean like the Rugrat?"

"I was thinking more like the *Hamilton* character."

Huh. "I haven't seen it."

"Oh, you've got to!"

Millie laughed. "One thing at a time, *Angelica.*"

Angelica beamed. The amount of unbridled joy on her face actually took Millie aback. After years of not feeling close to any of the people she was related to, she actually felt a connection for the first time. It was heady. A bit of a mind fuck, actually. She figured she'd have to think her way through it later.

In the meantime, Angelica looked ready to pass out from exhaustion. Millie changed her bedding and got her tucked in before pacing her living room, wondering what to do next. Or rather, knowing what she had to do next, but doubting if she actually had the stones for it.

The key for her beat-up old Corsa stared accusingly at her, and she sighed, snatching it up. A minute later she was heading out of the housing estate she called home and into the suburbs, down a road she honestly never thought she'd travel again.

At the end of her parents' long driveway, Millie parked and forced a series of deep breaths. She rolled her shoulders, slapped herself lightly in the face, and then went for it.

Having run scenarios in her head of what she'd say when someone answered the front door—the scenario varying depending on exactly who answered—Millie was pulled up short upon finding her dad in the garden, his head pushed halfway into a hedge.

"Nasty things," he muttered, seemingly to himself but at a volume that was at odds with standing alone near dusk, making Millie think he'd noticed her arrival and was actually directing his statement at her.

She stared at him, fidgeting with her car key as he pulled himself upright.

"Slugs," he clarified. "The bane of my bloody life."

Millie swallowed, not sure how to start despite her scenarios. She'd shifted through disbelief, rage, disappointment, annoyance, and had finally landed back on incomprehension. "How can you stand there and talk about slugs?"

Her father sighed. "What do you want, Mildred? You've come to extort money, no doubt. Or have you gotten yourself into trouble?"

There was the rage again. Coming threefold now, because if her dad knew her at all, he'd know his doorstep would be the last place on earth she'd ever show up if she was in 'trouble.' Secondly, Millie had never once taken money from her parents, not that she had ever been offered the chance. And in the third instance, she hated her full fucking name with a vengeance. Which, now that she thought about it, the fact that they had been unwilling to do so little as respect her wishes in shortening it had been a pretty big precursor to not accepting Angelica.

Millie opened her mouth to broach the topic of Angelica, but felt unsure about using the name. It was new, and almost felt like it had been told to her in confidence. Now she thought about it, Millie began to wonder if Angelica would be furious at her being here in the first place. She'd wanted to vent, yes. Maybe get some sense of satisfaction out of telling her parents how cruel they'd been. But it wouldn't change anything, so what was even the point?

God, why didn't I think this through?

Her dad was studying her face, his own expression having darkened, despite the outdoor lights having clicked on. "You're here about Max," he said.

Millie couldn't figure out if he'd known that the entire time he was making aggravating small talk, or had only just figured it out, but it hadn't been a question.

"I had a visitor earlier," affirmed Millie, approaching the topic on tip-toe.

Her dad raised his eyebrows. "He's with you, is he? I should have known."

"What the hell does that mean?"

"Language, Mildred," said her father, deftly not answering the question.

"Fuck off."

He actually staggered back a step, his carrier bag of slugs he'd handpicked out of the hedge swinging in one hand. "Excuse me!"

"No. I said fuck off. I can't believe you—" Millie forced herself to stop. "Actually, I can believe it. No matter how many times I expect you to be better and you pull shit like this, I never seem to learn."

He opened his mouth to object again, but was cut off by an all-too-familiar voice.

"Mildred," intoned the waif of a woman walking up the driveway towards them.

Millie grit her teeth, the car key now digging into the palm of her clenched fist, and turned to face her. "Mother."

"I thought it was you making a scene out here."

"A *scene*?" Millie felt her eyes almost bug out of her head. "Would that be more or less of a scene than you calling the fucking police and having them show up in a squad car to take a bogus fucking statement against your own child?"

"Oh, don't be tiresome."

Millie wanted to shake her. There had been a long time in her life in which she thought herself a violent person for all the horrible thoughts she had. At one point she'd considered seeking counselling for anger issues, but—almost like magic—such instincts had vanished the day and hour she'd left home on her eighteenth birthday.

She'd seen an Instagram post not long after, a faux inspirational quote something along the lines of 'Before diagnosing yourself with depression, first check that you don't in fact live with assholes.'

Nothing had ever rung so true.

"I don't care what you think of me," Millie said now, pressing ever on. It wasn't entirely true, but she was yet to find words that better explained where she stood in relation to the opinions of her parents. "But your daughter does."

"Suzanne?" asked her dad.

Millie glared at him. "You know who I'm talking about. You hurt her—you're *still* hurting her—but if you could just take your heads out of your asses for two minutes and consider how she might—"

"We never redecorated your room."

The rest of her diatribe lost in the interruption, Millie looked again at her mother. "What are you talking about?"

"Your room. We didn't change it after you left."

Am I having a stroke? What the hell has this got to do with anything?

"You could have it back," Mother continued. "Maybe we gave up on you too soon, but we could have another stab at it."

It took two minutes of silently standing in the dark driveway surrounded by slugs for the warped meaning to sink in. Her mother was offering an olive branch. Telling Millie she could move back in, at which point they'd try and be better parents.

The unspoken condition rang loudly in her ears. It was like being slapped in the face by a wall of sound.

They wanted her to turn her back on Angelica. To leave her out in the cold for some semblance of her former place.

It took everything within Millie not to throw up. Without another word, she walked, whole body shaking, back to her car and started the engine. She couldn't think. It felt like a struggle to breathe, even, but she made it home.

Millie thought she might take down the bottle of sherry and pour herself a glass to calm her nerves, but the half-formed plan halted when she opened her door and saw Angelica back on the two-seater, wrapped in the duvet and evidently waiting for her.

"You couldn't sleep?"

"I heard you go out."

"Oh." Millie set the car key down on the little shelf by the door. "Right, yeah, the walls are super thin here, sorry."

"How were they?" asked Angelica, cutting to the heart of it. Her eyes were red-rimmed and cheeks freshly blotchy.

Millie tried and failed for something to say.

Angelica sniffled. "That good, huh?"

Millie shook her head. "Fuck 'em. You're here now. You've got me."

More tears started at that, from both of them, and there would undoubtedly be many more to follow.

Angelica stood up and approached Millie, holding out her arms, duvet still around her like a cape. Millie stepped into the hug, feeling for the first time like she had a family.

"We'll figure this out," she vowed, stroking her sister's hair. "Come what may."

Nine Lives at Lunchtime

At Lila's school, they had a game where you went to almost push someone over, give them a startle, then hauled them back up at the last second.

"Saved your life!" you'd declare, and they'd laugh.

The teachers told them not to play. They said it wasn't very nice, or safe, but what did they know?

One sunny afternoon in May, Lila decided to add an extra layer to her fun. She ran about, trying to save nine lives during the lunch break. She got eight and decided on Jimmy for her final target. He'd be easy, because he'd always been small.

She ran up, pushed him down, but something didn't go quite right.

With arms empty and ears full of a terrible sound—bone on concrete—Lila saw there were no more lives to be saved.

Tried and Tested

It was officially way too early, at least according to Sandra's body clock. Her alarm clock had other thoughts on the matter, however. Insisting she got up for her daily dose of testing—and subsequent grief—before work, it buzzed. She silenced it. Rodger snored beside her, unstirred.

With a groan and a grunt, Sandra pulled herself out of bed and fumbled her way across the room to the en suite bathroom. This was always her least favourite part of the day, and not just because waking up seemed to be taking more and more energy these days. Energy she didn't have.

Taking a moment to look at herself in the mirror through still-drowsy eyes, she psyched herself up best she could. "Come on, Sandra," she murmured to her mirror-self, "You can do this."

Her reflection didn't seem so sure.

On autopilot, she took a clean, waxed paper pot from the stack and a corresponding white stick to put in it. Sitting down, she dutifully peed in the cup, just as she had been doing every day for three months.

Once, so far, she seemed to have ovulated, but there'd been nothing since. Of all her little testing strips, most stayed pale and disappointing except for that one that had a little colour.

Sandra went through the motions of dipping the testing strip, not sure how much more disappointment she could take. It took her a full ten seconds to register the vibrant, almost instantaneous response on the test.

She blinked at the strip, barely believing it could be true. According to her app, she wasn't supposed to ovulate for another week, and she hadn't had any period the previous month at all.

Too many times in the past, she'd got her hopes up only to have them dashed. Now, she forced herself to be sensible. Calm. Patient.

Not taking her eyes off the first test, Sandra lifted a second strip from the packet and repeated the dipping process.

Again, the result was instant: a strong positive.

Sandra almost dropped the sample cup. Composing herself, she disposed of the contents, finished up her business and washed her hands. The version of herself she saw in the mirror now looked more awake but anxious now instead of deflated.

She felt a little sick. But no matter, she braced herself and strode back into the bedroom proper. Sliding back into bed, she gave Rodger a gentle nudge with her finger.

No response.

She jabbed him in the ribs, and he sat up with a heaving breath and wild eyes. "What is it? What's wrong?"

"Nothing," said Sandra, feeling a little guilty for startling him.

Rodger's initial panic subsided a little, then turned into confusion. "What's going on?"

"I, uh… I mean, we…." She bit her lip.

Rodger sat up properly and put his glasses on. He gave her a considered look. "Sandra, honey, you don't look well." His eyes travelled to the right and Sandra saw the bathroom light reflect off his glasses. His eyes softened. "You did another test?" He sighed. "Well, you know, honey–"

She cut him off with a kiss, not able to contain herself or bear another rousing pep talk about how bad results were really okay and they'd get there in time.

Rodger put his hands on her biceps and leaned away. His face was a picture of surprise and concern. "Sandra, honey?"

"We need to have sex," she said. "Right now."

Rodger stared at her for a long second, then blinked twice. She tried kissing him again, but he stilled her. "Are you sure you're okay?"

God! He could be so infuriating. "I'm fine, I'm fine, let's just get it over with already!"

Rodger laughed despite himself. "You old romantic."

"I'm not joking," said Sandra, her mood thoroughly soured.

"No," said Rodger, his own expression sobering once more, "Clearly not. Are you going to clue me in, or—?"

"I'm ovulating!" said Sandra, the words coming out in a '*it's obvious you clueless bastard*' kind of way rather than the '*isn't this brilliant?*' she had been feeling five minutes ago.

Now, feeling foolish, Sandra had to force her enthusiasm. "Can we please just have sex?" she asked, mortified by the new tone in her voice: pleading.

"Well, I mean—" began Rodger, clearly flustered. "We can. Obviously we can. I just…." He paused to run his eyes over her again. "Are you sure you're up for it? You seem a little…"

He didn't have the heart to finish the sentence and Sandra was glad of it. Her own brain provided plenty of its own conclusions.

She seemed manic. Desperate. Crazed, and not at all attractive.

"I'm fine," she insisted again, careful to keep her voice even. "Look!" She proudly showed him the test, hoping that would make him understand. It really was the strongest positive result she'd ever seen, even from all the photos all the other women in the online support group shared. If anything, the test was stronger now than it had been when it was first dipped.

Rodger frowned at it and Sandra's heart sank in response. Why wasn't he doing a happy dance? Why wasn't he sweeping her up in his arms? She looked at the test again to make sure she hadn't somehow misread it. You'd think misreading a simple two-line test would be impossible, but she'd seen it done plenty of times in the online group. Some of the women convinced themselves there was a super-faint second line when clearly there was no reaction at all, taking what they wanted to see to the chat room for confirmation.

So many women didn't take the truth well. Sandra's heart broke for all of them. But that wasn't what was happening with her. The second line wasn't some almost-impossible thing to see here. Hers was clear as day. She wasn't going mad.

So why wasn't Rodger celebrating?

He took her hand, finally looking up from the test to meet her gaze.

Sandra tried not to cry. She knew she was being overly emotional and hated how unhinged it made her seem, even to herself.

"Sandra, sweetie," said Rodger, ever so gently, "Aren't your ovulation strips usually green at the end?"

She threw up her hands, beyond exasperated. "Why does that even matter right now?"

"So, uh… that's a yes?" Rodger pressed. "Usually green?"

"Yes!" snapped Sandra. She had never known her husband to be so difficult before. It was like he *wanted* to provoke her. "Asking pointless questions really isn't helping. If you didn't want me, all you had to do was…." She trailed off at the sight of Rodger sitting there, patiently waiting for the end of the outburst.

He wasn't laughing at her. He didn't look annoyed, or unmoved. In fact, he looked *extremely* moved. If Sandra wasn't very much mistaken, there were tears building behind his eyes too. It took all of the steam out of her sails. "What is it?" she asked, voice so quiet, scared.

"I…" said Rodger, clearing his throat. "I think you lifted the wrong test. They're beside each other in the cabinet, right?"

"The wrong test?" It took a minute for the suggestion to sink in, after which Sandra looked at the testing strip once more. She'd been so focused on the result, she hadn't paid much attention to the handle part.

The *blue* handle.

Sandra gasped, her right hand going to cover her mouth of its own accord. "I did the wrong test!"

Rodger smiled a little, but his eyes were terrified—like he knew what was coming next, but he was scared to say it out loud.

"I... I'm not—" Sandra stammered. "I'm not ovulating."

"No," said Rodger, a tremble in his voice. "You're—

"Pregnant," she finished, her own voice seeming far away. She was actually pregnant. She— Her brain caught up. "Oh my god! We did it!"

Rodger smiled and pulled her into a hug. Sandra had no objections when he insisted they go back to bed. Tomorrow, she'd get to reset all of her alarms.

Haste

Mama always said, "Less haste, more speed."

"Now, Genevieve," she would say. "Don't go rushing around so much. It's unladylike. And, what's more, the bad men will get you."

Genevieve chose to translate the advice as, 'don't get caught.' Which was altogether much easier to follow, because there wasn't much danger of that. Little time jumps weren't all that risky, really, and Geni was good at them. Plus, the Wild Hunt didn't scare her.

What Mama didn't understand was, certain situations just *called* for supernatural intervention. Like right now, as Geni headed to the bakery and could see there was only one peanut éclair left. Kristen was a little way ahead of Genevieve up the street, destined to reach the bakery first, and Geni just knew she would take the treat for herself.

Well, not on her watch. There was only a matter of metres in it, surely not enough of a displacement to set off the Hunt's trackers, scanning for magic use.

Geni made the jump, arriving at the front door just ahead of Kristen. She couldn't help but do a little dance. That éclair was hers!

She ran up to the counter and placed both hands on the glass, her mouth watering. Then she looked up, expecting to see the baker stood there, tongs in hand, awaiting her coin.

Instead, Geni was faced with the leader of the Hunt. He stood behind the counter, grinning through his skull mask at her.

"I have travelled for millennia, across many plains, and this day I finally come face-to-face with the mighty Chosen One!" He laughed, deep and throaty. "I knew you could not resist the pull of your magic for long. What is it you have to say to me now?"

Geni crossed her arms and blew her fringe out of her eyes.

"Well, crap."

Childhood Troubles

Maude was playing with her dolls on the dirt floor when she heard her father come in the back. Jumping up to go and greet him, she was stopped in her tracks—hand halfway to the door handle—when she heard him whisper something. To her mother, she assumed.

Drawing back her hand, Maude hesitated—knowing she shouldn't listen, knowing she'd be scolded if she were caught, but unable to pull herself away completely. Silently she stood, not going nearer and not backing away, locked in a stalemate with herself.

"They're going up the road," she heard her father say.

Her mother made an indignant noise. "Again?"

He didn't answer, but Maude imagined him nodding. The kitchen fell silent again, and she finally pulled herself away, to the window. The little farmhouse was back from the road but still within sight of it, if you strained your eyes.

Straining as much as she possibly could, Maude let out a frustrated huff. It was only trucks she saw out there. Hardly anything worth talking about.

"What are you doing, Maudie?"

She spun around and slapped her tiny palm down on her father's bare forearm.

"You shouldn't sneak up on people!" she scolded, using the most authoritative voice she could muster, but he only laughed which left her no choice but to stop frowning and look up at him with a wide smile.

Then, remembering, she glanced back to the window. The trucks were gone.

"Who—" she began to ask.

"The army," he said.

"Huh." She turned around again to sit on the sofa properly—feet dangling over the edge, wanting to ask if the army were goodies or baddies but resisting the urge.

"Daddy," she began instead.

"Yes, dear?"

"Will I understand things when I'm older?"

He sighed a little and took a seat beside her. "The older I get, the less I understand."

This didn't satisfy her, but she didn't push it. Her mother didn't like how many things she asked about, but her dad always tried his best, even if he didn't always know. She'd ask him an easy one, Maude decided: "What's for dinner?"

And his smile returned. "Let's investigate," he said, lifting her onto his back and carrying her to the kitchen.

A few months later, her mother gave birth to a baby boy—her second son. There were six of them living in the farmhouse, now. Her dad said he was planning to extend it, come summer, and there was talk of electricity coming to the area.

One of their neighbours came to visit when the baby—still unnamed—was just a couple of days old. Maude was watching him intently as he slept in his makeshift cot when she heard the knock. She glanced at her mother, who was sat in the rocking chair, reading.

"Aren't you going to answer it?" Maude asked, but she got no response. "Mother? Aren't you going to—"

"It's just Mrs Mills from down the road," said her mother, cutting off the question as if her words both answered and explained it.

Maude frowned and the knocking continued. "Would you like *me* to answer it?"

Her mother grunted. "Can't ever get a minute to myself," she muttered, making her way to the door and swinging it wide. "Ah, Mrs Mills! What a surprise. What can I do for you?"

Maude had followed her mother into the kitchen and was stood behind her long skirts, just peeking her head out enough to see two big eyes and an even bigger mouth—wide with a smile and no teeth to speak of—looking back at her.

"My, my," said the mouth. "Isn't this one growing up? She'll be chasing the boys 'round soon enough."

"She most certainly will not!" Mother snapped. "What do you want?"

"Oh," said Mrs Mills, her mouth hanging even more open. "Didn't mean anything by it, I just… nevermind. I brought a gift, for the babby."

Maude couldn't see her mother's face from where she stood, but she assumed her eyes had narrowed at talk of presents.

"Oh?" was all she said.

"Yes," said Mrs Mills, sounding excited as she handed over her parcel. "I hope you like it. Knitted it myself."

"It's very… thoughtful," said Mother. "I've got to get on making dinner now."

"Right you are," said Mrs Mills, as the door closed in her face.

Maude watched as her mother tossed the handmade blanket onto her rag pile, used for cleaning up spills.

"You don't like it, mummy?" she asked, confused.

"Of course I don't! It's an offence. Can't believe she had the nerve!"

Maude cocked her head to the side before making her way to the rag pile. "Is it––" she began, cutting herself off and then restarting the sentence afresh. "Is it because of the colours?"

Her mother ignored her, making her way back to the baby, so she assumed she'd got it right. Again she was aware of a nagging feeling, deep inside her, that there was something she was missing. How a beautiful new baby's blanket embroidered with orange, green, and white could be so bad.

It was the next year that the family got their first television set. Maude's mother would never let her watch it unaccompanied, and even *with* company she had a nasty habit of standing directly in her line of view— folding laundry or some such. That was until, one day, her mother was out shopping and her father had fallen asleep watching the news, meaning there was no one to censor whatever it was they'd been trying to keep from her.

Footage of explosions, gunfire, and fighting filled the screen. Her eyes—wide enough to drive a tractor through—might as well have been glued to it.

"Daddy," she said quietly, before becoming louder and more insistent. "Daddy!" She heard him stir behind her but still didn't look away. "Things have gone wrong, Daddy! What's happening?"

In a low, gruff voice that she'd never forget he said, "The Troubles."

Making no sense of it, she repeated the words over to herself. It was the first time she'd heard them, but it certainly wasn't the last.

Nature's Revenge

It was finally here—the day Kirsty had been preparing for all month.

She'd read all of the magazines she could on the topic, and all of the books from the library, too. Not all of the webpages, obviously, because that truly would be a never-ending task rather than just feeling like one. But she read some sites—maybe two dozen—and she made notes. Lots of notes. So many notes she could have written a book herself.

Then, after the general research stage, Kirsty's search got more specific. She had a list of the items she'd need, and a cross-referenced list of all the boxes each item needed to tick.

She didn't want just any bedding; she wanted a hypoallergenic set made from natural fibres. And she wouldn't settle for any old food; Kirsty wanted organic, locally sourced brands only.

So she took her time, sparing no expense, and gathered it all up.

She set up storage to keep all the supplies in, colour co-ordinated it, and made a wall chart of when she'd need to order more.

Kirsty had done every possible thing she could think of to get ready.

And then she'd finally bit the bullet.

She went down to the shelter, looked at all the cats and kittens, and looked again.

It was a long time before she found her—the perfect feline she'd been dreaming of.

Kirsty took her home.

She named her Twinkles.

She gave her food, and treats, and all the toys she'd gathered.

Affronted, Twinkles shat in her slipper and went to bed.

Babies and Broken Skies

Alina loved the baby. That, if nothing else, she knew for sure.

She watched the sky darken, threatening rain, and tried to focus on it and not the churning inside her.

The mum had the baby out in his stroller, rolling it back and forth in front of Alina's house as if she knew what torture it was to her and was inflicting it on purpose.

Didn't she care that it was going to rain, and the baby would get wet and cold, or that Alina had been trying—really trying—for more than a year and just couldn't do it, couldn't make her body work to the same result?

It was cruel. Alina decided that the mother was a right bitch and didn't deserve to have a little one. She cast her eyes to the clouds again, squinting at them as temptation warred within her.

It was safe to focus on the cool of the day. It helped her balance out the heat of her blood, for a while, but at the end of it, the tempest still raged.

She couldn't really do it, could she? Was it abduction if the child needed rescuing and was calling her? Wouldn't that make it a mercy mission?

The wind picked up, rattling the window, and the mum looked to see where the noise came from. Alina ducked from her line of vision.

The mum took the baby inside as the storm began in earnest.

At World's End

Living history doesn't go back so far these days, what with all the death around, but Mother says there might just be hope out there, somewhere. Animals on the other side of the mountain, or other people hiding out in secluded places, waiting for winter to finally end.

Inexplicably, and despite everything, she remained a steadfast fount of knowledge and encouragement.

Mother made sure I know how to live by numbers. Counting survival in concrete terms of cans and calories, the square footage of the underground bunker needed to store all that food, plus a few other essentials— candles and matches and a water purifier— leaving just enough room to breathe and move around.

I was ten when I realised the math was off. That she was holding out on me. Or— rather—holding out on herself for my benefit.

By her calculations, the cans should only last half as long as she'd said. But what I didn't factor was the giant hole in the equation: her absence. The truth of it only really sinking in when she set out her final set of instructions.

She'd taken the seeds from the very last apple—the last piece of fresh food we had—and I watched as she dug the frozen earth with a knife, her hands shaking as she made tiny holes near the roots of an old tree stump to put them in.

"Six to ten years to bear fruit," she said, "at least in ideal circumstances. This not being those…" She trailed off and smacked the earth extra hard with the flat of the blade, then turned and pointed at the bunker with the tip. "Just don't leave until you see green. Green means growth. Means life." *That there's a chance after all,* she didn't exactly say, but I heard all the same.

I shook my head, even as I stood there shivering under my four coats, wanting to tell her how pointless it was. I mean, six to ten years *minimum* for some apples? What was that when up against a winter that was already older than me?

But Mother looked at me—eyes as sharp as the knife she was wielding—and I swallowed the words, my stomach howling at their bitterness. I ran the math again, knowing that the cans would only last both of us three years if we stuck very closely to the one-a-day rule.

And then it clicked.

"You go back inside," she said. "I'll finish up here."

Again, I tried to argue—willed myself to fight with her with every last breath in my stupid, starving body—but she'd turned her back on me, focusing her attention on the seeds. The earth. The future.

"Close yourself in," she said, and I did, hating myself even as I set the lock. Hating her for making me. For always being right, and having facts and logic on her side.

I hated that she told me to walk away from her. That she stayed right there and left me alone. At night, the words still echo in my brain, but at some point they changed. Or maybe I did. Days and months and years ticked on, the stockpile of cans depleting all the time, and creation itself becoming recontextualised.

Go back inside. Close yourself in.

She was telling me to live. That my life was worth something. That she saw that, and treasured it.

I peeled the labels from the used cans and pulped them, making paper so I could write down everything she'd ever told me and turning the cans themselves into lanterns, hoping one day to have enough light to fill them all.

Go back inside.
Stay safe.

Keep living.
I love you.

I'm half-convinced that when I do finally make it back outside she'll still be by the seeds—maybe saplings, now—having used her own body as a windbreak, her flesh as nourishment.

It's not all that different from when she carried me. But she carried me. Is still carrying me.

I asked her if she ever regretted it, and she said, "No, never. Not once," which are words I use to keep me warm most days.

It feels like living history has halved, with her gone, but I'm still here. All of her sayings and quotes and wisdom—love, so much love—are still carried in my head. My chest. My gut. And now coming out of my fingertips in the flickering candlelight.

Keeping me going.

Because who knows? Maybe there really are people on the other side of that mountain. For Mother, I make it my mission to find out. One day and one can at a time. Until there's green again.

Until spring.

Triggers

"Shit!"

Gina heard a smack and a crunch and threw herself back, away from the sounds in the dark.

"Fuck!" Her hip went into the corner of her bedside table and her tailbone thwacked the floor as she landed. Hard.

There was a scrambling sound to her right, and the light flicked on.

She screwed her eyes shut, dazzled by the brightness, and focused on her breathing.

"Gina?" came a voice from the bed. Uncertain, and filled with sleep. Distant, and yet still far too close.

Gina flinched and had to restart counting again from the top. When she dared to open her eyes, the action sent two tears running down her face, one for each cheek. She scrubbed harshly at them with the back of her hand, furious with the sign of weakness.

Yes, she knew that was bullshit. That crying was sometimes necessary. That it often helped. She assured her clients of that all the time as they spilled their hearts in her office. But right then, she didn't care for the logic of it. She felt the dampness of her tears on her wrist and almost wanted to slice it off for how powerless she felt.

"Gina?" Ben asked again, and he moved over in the bed to look down at her.

She cringed away from his gaze. From her name on his lips. From the sight of blood, vivid scarlet, running over his lips and down his chin from where she'd struck him.

Gina looked down at her shaking hands and found his blood smeared across her knuckles, right beside the residue of her tears that had been bothering her a moment before. She was already over it. Had already shifted her focus.

"What happened?" asked Ben. "Bad dream?"

She nodded. "Nightmare."

He frowned, and she knew she didn't need to elaborate, but she found the words forming anyway.

"It was a bad one. A..." It felt like there was broken glass in her throat as she swallowed. "A memory. It..." *Shit, stop shaking!* "It was him."

Again, she didn't need to elaborate. Ben knew. Ben had always known.

"What can I do?" he asked, and the sound of his voice, gentle though it was, grated on her.

She shook her head, knowing that she should be sorry for hitting him—that she'd probably broken his nose, and that she'd undoubtedly be sorry later. That she'd be super tender and help him set it in a while— but not yet. She… *fuck.* She couldn't touch him yet.

"I need a minute."

He nodded once, the movement sharp, his jaw clenched.

Love fluttered in her chest at that. His unquestioning acceptance. The fact that he was mad—she could see it in his eyes, and could guess from what little she could see of him from her position on the floor that he was holding himself rigid, his hands probably in fists. But he wasn't mad at her.

Ben got it. Which is why she allowed herself to be with him. To trust him, when she stepped back from hugs from strangers and out of situations in which she'd have physical contact with others. Those were her boundaries, and he was the only one she let beyond them.

Except for times like this.

It flashed in her brain. A still image of the memory that had resurfaced in her nightmare, paired with the sound of his voice. Not Ben, but her attacker.

Ben's brother.

God, it had been how long? Years, now. Almost a decade, and this still happened. Hardly ever now, but evidently she wasn't entirely free yet. It was possible she might never be.

Gina closed her eyes again and breathed through the spike of panic in her blood. She was assaulted by more images of the nightmare—the memory—and forced herself to let them flow through her. They'd come into her brain, and if she didn't fight them or interact with them in any way, then they'd fade out again.

She heard Ben shift on the bed and assumed he was going to get a towel for his nose. He knew not to approach her. Not to make the first move.

When the sound of his padding feet disappeared into the bathroom, Gina pulled herself up off the floor and tentatively set herself back in bed. Her lower half already felt bruised from the fall, but she wasn't up for checking. If it was done now, it was done. Looking wouldn't undo the wounds.

Ben walked back into the room and gestured to Gina with the towel, a silent question.

She lifted her arm and he handed it over. She wanted a shower—to feel near-scalding water splash over every inch of her fast enough to almost wash her away—but at the same time didn't want to be alone, and didn't want anyone in the bathroom with her, so the towel would do.

She rubbed at her face first, then the blood on her knuckles.

"Can I sit?" asked Ben, and she nodded.

He settled himself at the far edge of the bed and waited, pointedly not looking at her. The first time this had happened, she'd screamed at him not to watch her. Even his eyes had felt like further violation. Which, again, she knew made no sense, but was true nonetheless.

Gina moved her thoughts to a different memory that twisted her up in a different way. Of Ben catching his brother, and them fighting. Of Ben knocking him down, and him not getting up again. Part of Gina felt like she shouldn't feel glad that he'd died—that she was better than that, even if he wasn't—but any guilt she'd felt was long gone now.

She knew Ben sometimes had his own nightmares, but he never told her about them. He'd been so messed up during the trial, but it had been ruled self-defence. There were "extenuating circumstances," said the judge, and he'd looked down at her with his kindly old eyes as he'd said it.

The verdict was of course a relief, but it didn't set anything right. Ben had broken down for a long while, and Gina shut everyone out—even and especially him—but somehow they found their way back to each other.

Gina reached out her hand, and he took it.

Ben shuffled closer, slowly putting his arm around her.

"Tighter," said Gina. "Hold me tighter." And he did.

The sun was coming up, and they didn't get back to sleep, but they held each other.

They got through it, one breath at a time.

My Sister the Space Cadet

She was the kind of person that stayed up on nights the clocks went back. As if it might forget to happen if she weren't personally there to witness it. Some people called her a control freak. They found her quirks annoying.

Not me.

Those other jerks were jealous.

My sister was the best. Always the top of her class. Always the highest achieving person at whatever she did. Never backing down from whatever she wanted to do, wherever she wanted to go.

She always wanted to be an astronaut. Or—no, that's not quite true. It's funny how the solid facts of a person can shift and fade afterwards. Time burning holes in memory.

My sister always wanted to be a time traveller. She *settled* for being an astronaut.

Except…

Except that, when she died, it was one of those nights. She was propped up, coughing. Keeping everyone else up, too, with the noise.

We sat by her bedside. All watched her tick off that one last task from her list.

My sister stopped breathing at 2.01 AM. And then, by the time we got the doctor...

Official time of death: 1.52.

The Change

Rena did not want to grow up. She was sure most kids felt some kind of apprehension about it but, for her, there was genuine fear. Ant that would be her parents' fault, insisting—as they did—on pulling her out of school on 'Sexual Health' days and delivering the talks themselves. God, it was awful!

Every teenager she'd ever known, either in real life or from TV, had a cringe-worthy story of their mum or dad fumbling through an awkward version of 'The Talk.' Whereas Rena had both her folks weighing in, and it wasn't just a one-off experience. She supposed it might have been okay if they had been professional educators or had a talent for explaining things, but mostly they excelled in making Rena terrified of her own body.

"You'll grow extra hair," said her dad.

"And you might be a wee bit more smelly," added Mum with a blush.

Dad grimaced but soldiered on. "If you've got any problems with the… um, *blood aspect*, your mum can help with that."

Mum nodded enthusiastically at that part.

Dear. Lord. Rena couldn't take any more of this. When her mum said, "Your nails will grow faster, and your teeth, too," she rolled her eyes skyward and gave it all up as a practical joke. It had to be, right? Except it wasn't funny. It was like her parents were from another freaking planet.

When Dad opened his mouth to say his next piece, Rena interrupted him to ask how much longer this was to go on. "I mean, you can't keep doing this every week until I'm eighty."

Her parents exchanged a look then turned to smile at her. "We just want you to be prepared, darling," said Mum. "But I get it. We maybe went a little over the top."

"*Maybe?*" repeated Rena.

Her dad winked at her. "Just a little."

"But the good news is that we're done," concluded Mum.

Wait. Rena sat forward. "Seriously? No more of these…" She trailed off, failing to find an adequate word to describe what could really only be classed as torture. "No more of *this*?"

Dad frowned. "There's no need to be so thrilled about it."

Rena forced the smile from her face. "Right, yeah. Sorry."

"Oh, my little girl is growing up!" exclaimed Mum, reaching for a tissue in her bag.

Dad squeezed her free hand in solidarity. "Hey, it's all right," he said to both of them. "Come next Saturday, it'll all be over."

Rena did a double-take. *Saturday?* she questioned internally. Were they actually predicting when it would happen? Could you do that? Good grief, had they found a way to track her cycle before it even started? If she'd thought she was scared before, it was nothing compared to now. Even so, she didn't say anything. There was no way she could bear the conversation to go on a moment longer.

A week passed with trepidation. Rena was in two minds over whether she actually expected the change to happen as scheduled or not, and if she was even glad for the potential heads-up.

Come Saturday, she stretched and rolled out of bed. She'd slept through most of the day, which wasn't like her. Were her muscles more achy than usual or was she imagining it? She definitely felt super warm.

Oh, god, she thought as she trudged to the bathroom. *I definitely feel different.*

She jumped when she caught sight of herself in the bathroom mirror. Holy hell, was that her? Suddenly it all made sense.

Rena stared at the reflection, lupine eyes looking back at her.

Planned

Jenny slammed her door and threw herself down on the bed. It wasn't ten seconds before she heard her mother's feet on the stairs. She sighed and sat up, bracing herself for round two.

Mum knocked once and then came on in, just like always.

"Now, Jenny," she began, hands on hips. "What's all this about?"

Jenny groaned. She could never understand why her mother never gave her space to cool down after an argument. "I already told you what it was about, but you don't listen to me!"

"Oh, I'm the one that doesn't listen?" said Mum. "I don't think you heard me when I said 'no' the first three times."

"But *why*?" said Jenny, hating the whine in her voice but feeling powerless to change it. This always happened and it never got any easier. All she wanted was a little freedom. She was sixteen, for God's sake! Was it really such a terrible thing to go to a party?

"It's too far away," said Mum.

Jenny scoffed. "It's the next town over. Barely ten miles!"

Mum frowned and didn't say anything to that, a clear sign she didn't have any real leg to stand on and was just being difficult for the hell of it. Normally, Jenny would roll her eyes and grudgingly accept it, because what else was she going to do? But this was the last straw. Abigail was her best friend and she was moving across the country. There was no way in hell Jenny was giving up on her last chance to see her.

"Just because you never had a social life!" she spat, standing to her feet to face her mum properly. "I know you were only my age when you had me, and you had to give up so much, but I'm not you. I'm not going to come home pregnant and I'm not going to keep living like a hermit, paying for your sins, just because you didn't plan me!" She was panting now, her cheeks hot.

Mum stood with her mouth open and tears in her eyes. Her lip wobbled. "Y-you think I didn't plan you?"

Jenny blinked at her, surprised by the sudden shock and misery painted across her mum's face. "I mean, didn't you?" she said, suddenly doubting what she'd always held as a certainty, though she'd never actually been explicitly told. "I mean, you were sixteen. Not with anyone. I just always kind of assumed." She shifted uncomfortably on her feet, now feeling like the worst shit in the world.

Mum came further into the room and swept her up in a hug, which lasted a long minute, until both of their breathing had calmed. They sat on the edge of the bed and Mum ran a hand through Jenny's hair.

"Of course I planned you, my gorgeous girl. I always wanted a baby!"

Jenny's heart fluttered. "You always said your mum didn't support you."

"That's true," said Mum, sighing. "Once I had you, I was on my own. But I don't regret a bit of it. Those four months I spent setting up for our new life were the most exciting in the world!"

Jenny laughed. "Four months?" she questioned, wondering at the weirdness of the joke.

"Oh, yes," said Mum enthusiastically. "Once I saw you, I immediately fell in love, but it took a little time to figure out how to make you mine."

Huh? Jenny leaned away a little, so she could look her mother in the eye again. "What do you mean?"

"Oh, well." She waved a hand, "You know, these things are complicated. I didn't want to get caught. I had to find a way to take you that people wouldn't immediately notice, and have a place set up for us to go away to, right away, until the fuss died down. It was not easy getting a flat as a sixteen-year-old, let me tell you! You think you've got it hard now, but just imagine doing it all with a newborn in tow!"

Jenny's mouth hung agape. Mum looked over at her and shook her head. "See?" she said. "This is why I don't want you going to that awful place. God forbid anyone spot some resemblance. We'd be done for!"

Ghost Walk

She'd been out of food for a week.

There had been a point when the reserves of motivation she'd been stockpiling and her dwindling reserves of supplies had intersected, marking out the best time to get groceries in, but those celestial events hadn't coincided with the payment of maintenance allowance she'd been expecting. So, now the situation really was dire, rather than just feeling it.

At midnight, some of the money from work she'd done earlier in the year dropped into her account. It wasn't enough to get a full shop in, but enough to cover the basics. She'd long given up hope of ever seeing that particular bit of revenue after the clients hadn't responded to her invoice and she'd been too nervous to follow it up, but clearly they'd received it after all.

Well used to feeling conflicting emotions, she ruminated over each of them as if they were newborn kittens in need of round-the-clock care, despite the fact that some of them had been with her long enough to be through most of their nine lives.

Concern over the missing maintenance allowance payment was growing fast, and the unexpected client payment was the newest addition to the litter. The two didn't so much balance each other out as make her queasy, her head and heart pulling in opposite directions at once, resulting in a tailspin.

She was grateful of the payment, of course, but it came to her with a set of twin anxieties that was altogether too much to handle. There was guilt that she'd ever thought badly of her client, and annoyance at herself for having given up on them so easily.

Dread filled her as the knowledge that she'd have to call up about the missing payment the next day settled in. And there was the pressing issue of having to leave the house to actually get some food in the meantime. Her belly rumbled, assuring her it couldn't wait.

Suddenly, the reservoir of motivation didn't seem quite so full. Even so, she drew from it, putting on a hat, coat, socks, and shoes over her pyjamas, and bolting through her front door before she changed her mind.

It was a good thing her local shop had 24/7 opening, making midnight dashes possible. And going so late usually meant there weren't many other shoppers, which was great. But there were the three streets between her house and the shop. Three dark, empty streets with faulty streetlights that sometimes weren't as empty as they first seemed.

At the intersection of streets one and two, there was a bar that seemed to be open just as constantly as the grocery store. She hurried past it at a speed that would get her out of the way quickly but wouldn't cause people to raise eyebrows if they saw her.

Sometimes, people would be stood outside, smoking. Sometimes there was nobody about at all, and sometimes the coast would be clear right until she was just beside the door—then it would swing open and people would spill out, the crowd swamping her. Sometimes she waited for it to happen, and then it didn't, which was almost worse.

On this night, her anxiety built and built until she worried she might faint from all the unnourished blood rushing around her slight frame. She didn't encounter anyone, but that left her heavy with adrenaline and nothing to do with it, meaning the edge never wore off even when she'd reached the relative safety of the store.

The ten minutes she spent inside were uneventful, but her heart rate ratcheted up regardless. For as long as she was outside her house, she wasn't safe, and she couldn't afford to forget that, even if things seemed well.

She was sure the beating in her chest was so loud that the other two shoppers or one of the staff would be able to hear it.

In the bread aisle, a younger man whose uniform marked him out as some kind of management was standing with a handheld device, scanning items. Worried about what he might think of how bedraggled she was, or what his reaction would be to the cacophony of noise exuding from her, she turned and took another route to the till, disregarding her need for a loaf.

Relief joined her cocktail of emotions once more when she saw the self-service checkouts were turned on and accepting card payments. It seemed she'd got through the ordeal of being out in public without having to interact with anyone.

There was an errant thought about her doing something wrong in the short walk to the doors, or just coming across as guilty or on edge on the security cameras, and a guard following her, putting his hand on her shoulder and demanding answers for her behaviour. She tried not to chase the thought, knowing it would lead to a spiral of much worse thoughts, like the therapist had said, but the cats inside her head were already on the hunt, and there was no dissuading them when they had prey in their sights.

Back outside, she walked past a ride-on toy by the entrance that made a beeping noise followed by the high-pitched canned laughter of children. She jumped at the sound and her heart went past overdrive and into all-out tremors.

Mouth dry and eyes skittering around to see if anyone had witnessed her startle, she mentally cursed the stupid thing for still being switched on when all the kids were long in bed.

Steeling herself, she hurried on, the electronic laughter manic in her ears, mocking her as it followed her into the night. She could still hear it when she was well out of earshot, her brain replaying the scene again and again.

She had been so busy kicking herself for the fright, she'd forgotten to be cautious about her approach to the bar. Three men were outside, one of them staggering across the pavement. The other two, who were also clearly under the influence but not to the same degree, began to whistle and laugh at her when she had to swerve to avoid their friend. It was all she could do not to drop her bag and break into a run but, finally, she was past them.

She kept walking, kept trying to focus on her footsteps and not get distracted by all the noise in her head. Her shopping bag was heavy, and she shifted it in her sweating palm.

Walking past an unlit doorway, she jumped a second time as a man's face suddenly shone out of it, illuminated by the lighter he'd flicked on and held to the tip of a cigarette. Her brief look at the face told her that it had seen her startle and was annoyed rather than apologetic about it.

Had she cried out, or was the yelp just in her head? Thoughts scattered, she couldn't tell—couldn't remember the events of even a moment before. The edges of her vision were blurry, and she prayed she wouldn't black out.

When was the last time she'd had a glass of water? The gnarled skin of her bottom lip cracked when she bit into it, and she tasted blood. Gagging, she would have thrown up if there had been anything in her stomach.

Torn between speeding up to get the last of the journey over with and slowing down to make sure she took proper care in looking ahead and watching out for potential hazards before they were upon her, she forced her feet to stay in rhythm, doing neither. The adrenaline was pushing her forward, but she was still dizzy, and it counteracted the desire to run.

One more corner, past the house that always smelt like weed, and she was outside her own home again, fumbling with the key. Her hands had gone numb, and it took three attempts to get the door open.

Once inside, she slammed it shut behind her and deflated against it, her appetite gone. Looking down at her small bag of shopping, she was overtaken by tears, knowing that it wasn't going to last long and that she'd have to go out and do it all again, soon. If she got more money, that is.

Some of her friends—back when she'd still had friends—had told her that her problems were all in her head, and they'd said it in a reassuring way, as if that made them unimportant, or easier to face, but she knew better.

You could leave a house if it was haunted, but what was anyone supposed to do when the spectres were on the inside of their skull?

Conclusions

"Why do you read so much?" he asked her one evening, out of the blue.

"For interest," she replied, not looking up from the page.

"And you find stories more interesting than people?"

"I do."

"Why?"

Finally he had her full attention. Carefully placing a bookmark where she left off, she looked around the room and gestured to the many rows of filled shelves before answering, "They give me everything I could ever want."

"Really?" he continued to press.

She was getting annoyed but decided it best to get the conversation over with, so she set her current novel aside and looked him full in the eye.

"The stories, they tell you of adventures you enjoy?" he continued. "The books make you feel as if you've experienced all these things first hand? All the things you read about, that happen to people that never existed, that's what you want?"

"Yes," she admitted, after a long moment.

"Ah!" he sat up, suddenly, "So you *are* interested in people. Are indeed terribly lonely, in fact."

His words were no longer questions, but she felt the need to answer them, to reject them with strong vehemence and to pour her anger on him for even suggesting them.

"How on earth do you draw that conclusion?" she snapped, and he grinned before moving towards the door.

Just as he was about to slip out he turned and said, almost under his breath, "Because all you ever read is love stories."

Same Old Brand-New Self

Jessica could not believe the situation before her. It wasn't the plan. Or, at least, hadn't been her Plan A in a long time. She was already halfway through the rest of the alphabet, while her fool of a long-term boyfriend, Barry, played catch up, as ever.

After six years of dating, five years of Jessica dropping not-so-subtle hints at him to surprise her with a shiny rock for her finger, and four-and-half years of hopelessness, after having given up on the idea and convincing herself that she'd never *really* wanted to marry him anyway, all the while plotting the best way to get back at him for the slight, Jess sat in the middle of the crowded restaurant with her mouth hanging open and her eyes locked onto the small, pale blue box set in his outstretched palm.

Barry swallowed and looked around him, no doubt hoping she'd say something so he could get up off the floor and stop putting strain on his bad knee. Jessica was not merciful to his plight, however. He'd dared to keep her waiting? Well, she'd show him!

"I don't know," she said, pursing her lips as she considered pulling out her phone to double-check her horoscope. The thing was, she'd only come along on the date because she'd planned on ending things, and now she was faced with this. *Annoying Barry, messing up her plans.*

Plans were everything to Jessica. Above all, she loved to learn about and challenge herself, working projects and trying new things. She loved fresh starts, which usually involved the end of old things; hence the intended breakup.

At the start of this year, the plan had been simple yet far-reaching—so said the book she'd bought about it, complete with money-back guarantee! It was all about saying yes. Repeatedly. To everything.

Come what may, Jess was going to open herself up to a world of new opportunities with the power of a single word. She couldn't wait. Except, of course, she had, because she'd finished the book at 9.45 on New Year's Eve, and it simply didn't make any sense to start before midnight. Then, on January first, it hadn't made sense to implement the new resolution until she'd swiftly opted out of the sales pitch from a needy telemarketer. And now here went Barry, testing her. What a trying man!

A quiz Jess had done the previous week said her strength was planning (duh!), and her main weakness was being closed-minded (what?). Usually Jessica lived for quizzes, considering their results to be almost divine. But close-minded? That was just crazy talk.

She'd seriously considered writing to the magazine to tell them someone had made an error with the piece before deciding she would take matters higher up instead. She would prove to the universe itself just how open she was to, well, everything. Everything and anything that might come her way. Totally. One-hundred-percent—just so long as it was part of her plan.

It would be a breeze. She was *already* so open, after all. That's why she'd bought the book. And hey, if it didn't work out, then she could start saying no to things soon enough in the name of Lent. Lent was always a plan she did well with.

Would she give up chocolate again this year? She took another bite of her dessert as she considered it. But, oh yes, there was that other decision she had to make first.

"What do you mean, you don't know?" asked Barry, his voice straining as he tried to emphasise the question while also trying to not draw any more attention to himself. Fat chance there was of that. He was still knelt in the middle of the floor, his face turning an unflattering shade of red as waiters rudely pushed their way past him.

Jessica rolled her eyes, horrified that he would do this to her.

As she continued to chew on the question at hand, an errant part of her brain reminded her that she was already eighteen hours into her Yes plan (not counting the twenty-second break she'd taken when someone asked her for money on the street outside). But what to do when her plan to say yes interfered with her resolve to start the year as a single lady once more? It was impossible!

Except, now she thought about it, she was pretty sure there was a book further down her Amazon wish list about the power of saying no. That might be a better plan for her, given the circumstances.

"No," she said, finally.

"No?" repeated Barry.

"No," she affirmed, content that it was the answer to everything.

Barry blinked at her before trying and failing to get to his feet.

Jessica shook her head. He'd probably let his leg go to sleep, the fool. It would be good for her not to be saddled with him anymore.

No, she would be free. She'd go home, buy that book—because she deserved it, after such a tiresome day!—and then maybe break her Facebook Fast to let the world know about her exciting new plan.

At least until Lent.

The Swindle

I had this system for getting exactly what I wanted out of people. Okay, so maybe less of a system and more of a concept. It kind of boiled down to a single word: blackmail.

The genius of it came to me when I realised that I didn't even need to have any real dirt on anyone, I just needed to *pretend* that I knew something awful. The person would always fill in the blanks by themselves.

"I know your dark secret," I would say, casually picking my nails.

"What?" they'd say, and they would laugh.

I would give them this look—the first time, I practised it in the mirror for a week, but it's natural now—and they'd stop laughing and glance around.

"You're serious? But…but how did you know?" they would stammer.

And I would shrug and say, "That's not important now. The main thing is what you're going to do about it."

Sure enough, we'd cut right to talking about terms and I'd end up walking away with half the person's life savings or some treasured possession I could flog for a few quid.

This girl—the one in front of me now—is different, though.

"I know your dark secret," I said.

And she beamed at me. "Oh, really? Did you read my blog? I'd love to know what you think."

I blinked at her. "I—uh, I mean, what?"

She looked crestfallen. "You didn't read the blog?"

And she looked so sad that I found myself saying, "Oh, your blog. Right. Yes. Sorry, I misheard you."

And she brightened up again, telling me all the finer details of what she had apparently confessed to the internet the day before.

The story was so tragic, I ended up donating my life savings to get her back on her feet.

Last Being First

I can't believe I'm doing this.

I'm standing at the top of a cliff, ready to dive off into freezing cold water, and I'm maybe more scared than I've ever been in my life. But she's beside me.

I turn to her, watch the wind whipping her hair back from her face, and shake my head. "I can't believe I'm doing this!"

She smiles at me so bright, it feels like something unlocks within my chest, but the next moment, I remember why that part's locked up in the first place and try and shove the door closed again.

Looking away from her, I jump.

The water feels colder than I even imagined, but only for a second. What follows is another second that seems paused––could really have been a year or a lifetime––and I'm numb. And I'm floating.

There's movement in the corner of my eye. I look and she's there again, floating right alongside. She takes my hand and pulls me towards the beach. I'm not sure I want to go. For a minute, I almost resist the pull of her. But, well, not being able to resist her has always been part of my problem.

On the shore, she's panting. I can't stop looking at her, at the way her clothes are tight across her body, weighing her down. The way her chest is heaving. She's looking back at me, smiling again, and I know more than ever before that I'm in too deep.

I can't do it. I turn away, fight her off when she grabs for my hand again.

Last night, I stayed at her house—her on the bottom bunk, me on the top. I asked her why her bedroom was done up like she was twelve, and she said it had been decorated when she *was* twelve and they'd never really thought about changing it.

I don't know why, but I fixated on that. I guess it blew my mind that some things, for some people, hadn't changed in the past six years when everything seemed to have shifted for me.

Back when I was twelve, I was happy. I don't know when that changed—I'm not sure it was all at once—but now I can barely remember what it was like at all. I think I miss the certainty of it most.

"Laura," I said, biting my lip.

"*Kelsie*," she replied, mimicking my serious tone and then laughing.

The reaction almost made me back out of what I was going to say. I felt the words begin to dry out on my lips but, somehow, I took a breath and they floated out towards her.

"Laura, I… I think I'm going to kill myself."

She was silent. I waited. Then, when she still didn't make a sound—didn't laugh again or move or say anything I looked over the side of the bed to make sure she'd heard me and hadn't just fallen asleep or something.

She was looking back at me.

"You want to die?" she asked, finally, and it was almost like there was hurt in her eyes, but I'm not sure if I imagined that.

"No," I said after a long minute, my head suddenly starting to spin. "I don't want to die, I just…." My voice got real quiet. "I'm just not sure I know how to live."

"Oh," she said. She sat up.

After one more minute, I climbed down the ladder and sat beside her, our knees touching. When she opened her mouth again, I thought she was gonna yell at me or tell someone what I'd said. Panic rose in my throat as I wondered what they'd do with me if they knew—everyone else. My parents. Would they lock me away? Would they stop me? Did I want that? My head spun so fast I thought I was going to throw up and I was torn between surprise that I was feeling anything and worry at how ugly my vomit might make Laura if I puked on her sweater.

I was always worried about staining her, somehow.

She wasn't looking at me as she asked, "When?"

I blinked at her. "What?"

She turned her face so our eyes met. "When did you think about doing it?"

"Oh. I…." I had to look away from her. All of my words had gone missing. All of my reasons were right in front of me, but it was like I couldn't reach for any of them when I had this one new, big question in front of me, too. And it was so small, as well. Four letters that would have made me hate her, if that were possible.

When. That had been what she asked. Not why. Not anything else.

"When?" I stammered. It was on the tip of my tongue to say, 'I don't know,' but in that instant, I made a decision. I looked back at her and said, "Tomorrow."

That was the first time she took my hand. She pulled me over to her tiny desk and didn't let go as she dug around in the drawers for a pen and notepad before eventually dragging me back to the bottom bunk.

"What's this for?" I asked, scared of the answer. Was she gonna get me to write a suicide note? Would that help?

"It's a list," she said. "What should be number one?"

I looked at her like I'd never seen her before; like I hadn't spent three years stealing glances at her, wondering if she could ever feel about me the same way I felt about her. I felt stupid. Then I felt angry. I wanted to rip the notepad out of her hands.

"Pros and cons," I spat. "Is that it?"

She rolled her eyes and smiled, putting me on the back foot, my anger back in my pocket. "No, silly. We should make a list of what to do."

"What to do?" I repeated. "What do you mean?"

I already had a plan for how to end it. I had several, actually. Should I tell her that? Would it matter? Suddenly I found myself wanting to hear what *her* ideas were. I tossed out all of my own, wanting nothing more than for that conversation to last forever.

She was already busy scribbling when she said, "If you're gonna have one last day alive, you should make it good. What do you want to do?"

Again, I blinked at her. I opened my mouth but didn't know what to say.

"I think you should try base jumping," she said, carrying on in a casual, almost perky way as if she hadn't just blown my mind. "You know the cliff overlooking the pier? It would be perfect for it. We could get the train into town and maybe grab an ice cream beforehand and go shopping after. You know, for warm clothes? I'll buy you a burger. There's a carnival in Red Rover, I think."

On and on she babbled about all these plans for my 'perfect last day,' and all I kept thinking was how cruel it was that she was making me fall even more in love with her even now. *Especially* now.

"So, you'll do it?" she asked, looking up at me from her list for the first time in maybe an hour, her eyes bright.

"You'll be with me?" I replied, not willing to commit myself to an answer until I had hers.

And she smiled at me like sun splitting the trees, and I didn't know how to process any of it—how she could make my world feel okay and break my heart all at once. We'd have the perfect day and then it would just be… what? Over. All of it. Just like that? The thought resolved me. I knew then that it was the right call—that I couldn't go on when the sun went down and she walked away.

We fell asleep lying on the bottom bunk, my knees bent and pressed against the crook of hers; my arm around her waist, holding onto her like a life raft.

And now I'm looking out at the sea, drowning, and I can't let her hold my hand again knowing that if she takes it back, I won't be able to breathe and that she couldn't possibly hold on forever even if she wanted to.

I turn away. Her hand goes to my shoulder instead and I feel the heat of her skin, warm with adrenaline, through the wet cotton of my T-shirt.

"Come on," she says, and I follow like a bug transfixed on a fire, not really knowing myself or my actions. She sounds grave for the first time. For a minute, I think she's gonna tell me that she's the one that can't do it—that she's gonna give up and go home early, leaving me on the beach because she can't bear to stick around long enough for the sun to set.

I regret not letting her take my hand.

I'm looking at how many rings she has on, my eyes focusing on the flecks of glitter in her nail polish. The faint, faded lines on her knuckles where she tried to give herself a homemade tattoo, once, at the back of an unattended English class.

PEACE, she carved into one hand. *LOVE*, she wrote on the other. They were mostly healed up, the messages now little more than a ghost on her skin. I'm looking at them, forcing myself not to risk catching her eye and telling myself I won't cry in front of her if she goes now. I'm staring so intently at all the little lines on her hands that I don't notice at first when they get closer.

Her arms are around my neck and lips pressed against mine before my mind registers that she's moved and that she's no longer ahead of me but beside me, locked together with me. My lips move with hers all on their own and I can taste the salt from the sea on them. I don't know how long it lasts, but when we come up for air, I am breathless and panting and *alive*.

"Promise me," she says, looking so deep in my eyes I think she must know my whole life. Her fingers tighten around mine, her rings biting into the bone of my hands. "Promise me you'll still be here when I get back from holiday. Say you'll be here at Christmas, and Easter, and all the other breaks I get a chance to come back for."

I open my mouth and am just about to say that I will, that I'll promise her anything––*do* anything—but she shakes her head as if rethinking the request. My heart falls to the pit of my stomach and I think I feel the water I swallowed starting to come back up.

"Come with me," she says instead, looking nervous as if I were about to say no––as if I *could* say no. And I shake my head and smile at her and don't say anything because I don't know how to make the shape of words with my mouth while everything inside me is screaming, yelling that you can't save a person—not like that—and not caring that probably, someday, when she's at uni and I'm holding her back, we'll fall apart and I'll be right back here where I started. Alone.

"Come with me," she says again, the words a whisper on the wind. A plea.

And I do. I take her hand and go with her because how in the world could I ever say no, no matter that there's gonna be a when, not an if, in our future?

It sank in as we walked the rest of the way up the beach—that I had a future, that I *wanted* a future.

That this was the first day of the rest of my life.

Acknowledgements

'Earworms' was first published by Visitant Lit in February 2020.

'Prepared' was first published by Reflex Press in December 2021.

'Quest' was first published by Friday Flash Fiction in July 2019.

'Robin' was first published by Alpha Female Society in June 2021.

'Wingman' was first included in Hidden Voice Publishing Anthology: Volume Two (2020).

'Tangled' was first published by Scarlet Leaf Review in November 2020.

'Haste' was first published by Friday Flash Fiction in August 2020.

'Childhood Troubles' was first included in North Star: Short Stories and Poems by Female Northern Irish Writers (2020).

'At World's End' was first included in Worlds Within Worlds: Belfast Writers' Group Anthology Three (2022).

'Ghost Walk' was first included in Ghosts in the Glass: Belfast Writers' Group Anthology One, Second Edition (2017).

'Last Being First' was first included in Hidden Voice Publishing Anthology: Volume Two (2020).

Many, many thanks to each of these publications for including my work. And thank you, as always, to my wonderful editor Bridget Engman Wilde.

Trigger Warnings

Adult Language (Swearing): Triggers

Assault: Triggers

Body Horror: Earworms

Death/Grief:
Prepared, Nine Lives at Lunchtime,
At World's End, My Sister the Space Cadet

Fertility Issues:
Drawbacks, Tried and Tested,
Babies and Broken Skies

Gaslighting/Emotional Abuse:
Tangled, Dynamics

Mental Illness: Caretaker, Ghost Walk

Sectarianism: Childhood Troubles

Suicidal Ideation:
Drawbacks, Last Being First

Transphobia: Dynamics

CPSIA information can be obtained
at www.ICGtesting.com
Printed in the USA
BVHW032322140223
658501BV00004B/120